Gone to
IDAHO

Enid E. Haag

Gone to IDAHO

The Second Book in the New Mexico Gal Series

Copyright © 2017 Enid E. Haag.

All rights reserved. No part of this book may be used or reproduced by any means, graphic, electronic, or mechanical, including photocopying, recording, taping or by any information storage retrieval system without the written permission of the author except in the case of brief quotations embodied in critical articles and reviews.

Archway Publishing books may be ordered through booksellers or by contacting:

Archway Publishing
1663 Liberty Drive
Bloomington, IN 47403
www.archwaypublishing.com
1 (888) 242-5904

Because of the dynamic nature of the Internet, any web addresses or links contained in this book may have changed since publication and may no longer be valid. The views expressed in this work are solely those of the author and do not necessarily reflect the views of the publisher, and the publisher hereby disclaims any responsibility for them.

Any people depicted in stock imagery provided by Thinkstock are models, and such images are being used for illustrative purposes only. Certain stock imagery © Thinkstock.

ISBN: 978-1-4808-4626-5 (sc)
ISBN: 978-1-4808-4624-1 (hc)
ISBN: 978-1-4808-4625-8 (e)

Library of Congress Control Number: 2017906517

Print information available on the last page.

Archway Publishing rev. date: 10/16/2017

In memory of my pioneering Idaho Grandparents

Preface

• • • • • • • • •

Gone to Idaho is the second volume of the *New Mexico Gal* trilogy, a family saga. It continues the adventures of fifteen-year-old Emma, now almost grown, devoted to her papa and striving to build a life for both of them without the other two family members, Mama and brother Edmund. When Papa takes off to track down someone who might be his lost wife, Emma follows. Thus begins the next poignant tales of a strong-minded young woman unafraid to face the challenges and biases of early twentieth-century western frontier life in Colorado and Idaho, complicated by budding romantic attachments.

Chapter 1

• • • • • • • •

Santa Fe, New Mexico
1911

Emma watched as a lone cowboy ran to catch the daily Chili Line train leaving Santa Fe just as the conductor shouted, "All aboard." The door slammed, and the conductor waved through the half door to the engineer ahead that all were aboard. The train whistle blew twice before the cars lurched and slowly began moving out of the station.

The last passenger walked down the aisle, rolling with the motion of the train past several vacant seats before reaching the row where Emma sat. Motioning to the seat beside her he asked, "*Amigo,* is this seat taken?"

He was tall but bean-pole thin. She recognized him instantly.

"You know darn well it isn't taken, Juan."

He tossed his blanket roll into the overhead rack next to hers before sitting down and tipped his Stetson back a trifle with one finger. Emma saw him smile before he turned to her. He whispered, "Thought you'd leave without me?"

"What are you doing here?" she hissed.

"I have my reasons, Emma. You forget I know how you think. Fool me once but never twice."

Emma muttered, "You weren't asked. I don't need you."

"I'm here, and I plan to follow you like a faithful sheepdog."

"I can take care of myself," was her angry retort as Emma folded her hands on her lap.

"Yeah, just like you did once," snickered Juan, settling into the seat beside her. "You were pretty happy to see those sheepherders who found you when you attempted to run away after the court awarded custody of you to your Texas uncle."

Fighting to contain her anger over his chiding her about her failed runaway attempt years ago, she twisting sideways, away from him, to stare out the window at the rocky hillside supporting scraggly cedar and piñon bushes. She'd chosen the Chili Line over the more direct route to Denver in hopes that none of the family would be watching this local narrow-gauge rail line that transported supplies and a few passengers to small communities along the line to Antonio, Colorado. *Darn Juan!* He'd read her mind.

"I'm coming with you. We'll be two amigos looking for work in Idaho. There's nothing wrong with that, is there?" he asked, raising his voice slightly at the end. He turned from her and glanced at the nearby passengers, mostly ranch hands returning from a weekend in town, along with a few Navajos heading home after selling their pottery, jewelry, or blankets at the town market.

"Think you've got it all figured out, don't you, you smart aleck twenty-year-old college kid," said Emma.

"Just two men, one Anglo and the other Spanish, traveling together. Really! Someone's certain to report us to a sheriff. Why couldn't you leave well enough alone and let me search for Papa by myself?"

Emma's comment drew his attention back to her. "Fifteen-year-old young ladies don't travel alone. You know that. I couldn't let you. But you did solve one problem by deciding to disguise yourself as a man," chuckled Juan, slouching slightly in his seat and crossing his arms. "It will be easy for us to pass ourselves off as ranch hands seeking work. Oh, by the way, wonderful choice to travel to Antonito rather than directly to Denver. Brilliant thinking."

Exasperated at the turn of events, none of which she'd anticipated, Emma spat, "La-di-da." *Why does Juan consider me his responsibility?* she wondered. Turning toward the window in time to see the train cross the Rio Grande toward the Pajarito Plateau at the foot of the Jemez Mountains, she recalled occasions when Papa had brought her and Edmund up here in search of Indian artifacts. Those had been happy times, away from Mama's constant criticism. Papa allowed her to dig wherever she wanted and collect anything that caught her fancy.

"Why don't we call a truce?" urged Juan. "I'm here. Can't we look at this as our first out-of-state adventure?"

Ignoring his remarks, Emma stared out at the passing desert. She knew she was pouting but didn't care; he deserved the silent treatment. As the train crawled up the grade, she began thinking about her trip eastward with Senor Caruso from California after the earthquake. She'd been devastated by the loss of her family, so much so she'd lost her voice and had to communicate with the sign language Caruso taught her. That train had chugged along much like the one she now rode on. Caruso, who loved cartooning, had drawn a series of funny-looking trains huffing and puffing to climb the mountain passes. He'd even sung little ditties about a chugging engine, and members of the Metropolitan Opera Chorus, who were traveling in their car had joined in. How she wished Caruso sat next to her now rather than Juan.

Turning toward Juan, she found him slumped with his Stetson over his face, sound asleep. "Humph!" He didn't care enough to even stay awake. She quietly stood up and started to slide past him.

"Going someplace?"

"Yes, to find another seat with a more congenial passenger," she retorted.

"Well, partner, now that you're speaking again, shouldn't we discuss our travel plans?"

Arms crossed, Emma sat back down, staring into Juan's jet black eyes. "You're not coming with me," articulating each word carefully.

In a firm but calm tone, Juan asked, "What do you want to be called? I certainly can't use your real name without betraying your gender."

"You're heading back home, so you won't have to call me anything."

"Now look here, Emma, you can't stop me. I'm your sidekick. There's no arguing. I'm here, and I'm traveling with you. Two searching for someone is better than one." Juan's piercing, dark eyes stared into Emma's with determination. It was as if they were playing a game of who would flinch first. She strained not to look away. This challenge had to be won. The seconds passed, and neither gave in. Emma suddenly lost her concentration, blinked, and looked away. Slapping her knee with one hand, she vented her frustration. "Darn you. You always could stare me down."

Juan showed no jubilation but whispered, "Have you a name you'd like to be called?"

Resigned for the moment, Emma shrugged her shoulders. "I guess Gilbert."

"Gilbert it is," said Juan, lifting his right hand toward her to shake on the deal. Emma turned to offer him her hand. "We've just cemented a man-to-man deal." Juan winked.

The two watched the hilly scenery as the train wound its way northward. Emma felt herself relax. Right from the beginning, she'd had an uneasy feeling about traveling alone. Now Juan had joined her, she admitted to feeling less worried. But she certainly wasn't going to tell him that. Emma wondered why she'd caved in so readily. Normally, she gave as good as she got. Did she have another reason for letting him win? Could she admit she was stubborn and argued out of pure spite? Managing her Papa's store for the last year had taught her to be determined, to stand up for herself. If she didn't, no one else would.

Glancing at Juan beside her, she couldn't help notice him observing her lean legs beneath the tight jean pants. He normally only saw her in pants when they went riding, and then he didn't have much time to scrutinize her figure. She smiled to himself as she recalled how his hand felt on her bottom when he'd boosted her up into her pony's saddle when she'd first learned to ride at Uncle Fritz's ranch. She'd been slightly roly-poly then, but now all the baby fat was gone; she was skinny and flat chested.

Midmorning, Emma shared sandwiches, cookies, and coffee with Juan. Leaning back in his seat with half of a cup of java, he turned toward her and said, "You know, I've never really known how you all got separated from your mama. Do you recall what happened the day of the earthquake?"

Emma chewed and swallowed the last bite of her oatmeal cookie before emptying her cup. "Even though I was only ten at the time, the events of that day are imprinted in my memory. After Papa carried me safely out of the hotel, he ran back to get Edmund and Mama. They were to follow us, and when they failed to appear Papa ran back to find them. He'd just disappeared when Mama and Edmund emerged from the building. They hadn't seen Papa on their way out. We waited a long time, but he never returned, and Edmund decided to look for him. It wasn't long before the buildings around the hotel and then the hotel itself burst into flames. When the navy broke through the rubble blocking our street, they created a path and led us to safety. While I was watching them, I forgot Mama. From the time she'd exited the hotel with Edmund, she'd been acting strange, like she was in shock. Anyway, while I was distracted, she ran into one of the burning buildings near the hotel. That's the last I saw of her."

"So that's why your papa took off suddenly to look for her. For the past five years, he's thought she was dead, but now there's hope she might be alive. I'd do the same if I thought I could find my lost wife." Looking carefully at Emma, he added in a hushed tone, "Kinda like me trailing after you." Juan started to put his hand around Emma's shoulder but stopped himself. She was now Gil, a young man, beside him, not Emma. "I'm so sorry. I never knew."

Wiping moisture from her cheeks with a sleeve, she turned toward him. "Thank you. I've always blamed myself for her disappearance. I tried to run after her, but Caruso stopped me from entering the burning building. He saved me. He became my self-appointed guardian after that. While we waited for a train eastward, he and Martino, his manservant, searched everywhere for my family, but they couldn't find anyone fitting their descriptions. They even checked every merchant ship leaving the harbor, except one called the *Maryjane*, headed north up the coast toward Seattle. Nothing!"

Chapter 2

• • • • • • • •

Five Years Earlier
May 1906, San Francisco

Jamie looked up from the glass he was drying to see his best friend enter the bar and saunter toward him. "Top of the afternoon to you. What will it be, black coffee or a beer?" he asked, noting a little late Dillion's bloodshot eyes and grungy appearance. "A whiskey with dash of Dr. Johnson's then," he said, turning toward the large, cracked bar mirror.

"Don't bother. Nothing will help, not even Dr. Johnson's Elixir. Are you ready to clear out of this hellhole of a town yet? I am. Or are you still playing Sir Galahad to lost and frightened ladies?" asked Dillon, smiling lopsidedly at this friend.

Placing a whiskey glass with a splash of the special elixir on the counter in front of his pal, Jamie rested the palms of his hands on the edge of the bar and leaned toward his friend. "Try this. And no, I have my hands full with the one lady, thank you."

"Well then, let's get out of San Francisco, pronto,"

Dillon remarked before taking a gulp of the drink before him and heading for the door.

"Okay, I agree we should go, but I'm taking my lady with us," announced Jamie. He tried to hide the pleasure that flickered across his face as he watched his friend turn abruptly and walk back toward him.

"Jamie, you can't be serious about taking that strange woman with you. That's nonsense," said Dillon, flopping down on the barstool in front of his friend, who remained behind the counter. He set his square jaw; his bloodshot eyes looked directly into the intense blue eyes across from him. He added, "Think what you're taking on! She remembers nothing before the earthquake, not even her name."

"I know. I know it doesn't make sense," Jamie responded. "But look at it this way—I've delayed leaving San Francisco for two weeks to try to locate someone who can identify her, with no luck. Rescuing her from the building next to the Palace Hotel while it was ablaze bestowed responsibility. I may not be much of a practicing Christian, but I know my Christian duty to a fellow human being. Have you ever wondered why I happened to be passing at the very moment she was terrified and couldn't help herself? I didn't usually walk that way. Why did I then? I've ask myself that question a thousand times. Perhaps I was meant to be there for her at that moment, not only for her salvation but for mine too.

"No, I just can't abandon her. The city's a mess. There's no local law or government except the military. Everything is centered on taking care of the injured and the homeless, not reuniting families, especially the nameless. Other than a few burns that are healing nicely, she suffers only from temporary memory loss. All she has is me, a footloose bartender seeking a future. It's not in my nature to abandon ladies in trouble. I kinda like the idea of being a knight in shining armor, saving a lady in distress," smirked Jamie, straightening up to his full height.

"You're already her 'knight'—you saved her from the fire. Isn't that enough? She doesn't have to be your forever responsibility. Leave her here. I'm certain the navy boys will take care of her," argued Dillon.

"Yes, that's just what I'm afraid of, a roving-eyed sailor or some other nut picking her up and doing what they will with her. No, I can't have that. She's a real lady. All she needs is time to recover from the shock of the earthquake and fire. I'm going to give her that time away from the sights and sounds that keep bringing back the horror. I'm taking her with us to Idaho."

"Have you searched everywhere for anyone who might recognize her?"

"Of course I have," came his angry retort. "I've searched the tent city, the hospitals, and talked to several naval personnel. I checked with all the bartenders with whom I'm acquainted. Nothing. I've put up notices. No response. There's such chaos in the city. I'm not surprised I'm not hearing anything. Everyone is intent on survival. Those who can are leaving Oakland by train, but tickets are hard to come by. I heard that the Metropolitan Opera Company got lucky early on, transported east because Caruso was among the musical troupe. Being a celebrity counts, you know. We peons don't."

Sliding off his stool, Dillon turned back toward his friend. "How do you plan for us to travel north? The trains are only running east and west by order of the president, and only a select few can purchase tickets."

"Easy. I located a ship that's leaving for Seattle. It happens to have space for the three of us but only one cabin, so you and I will be sleeping on deck while our lady occupies the cabin. It's not ideal, but it will get us out of here."

"Chivalry isn't dead with you, my friend," chuckled Dillon, waving as he exited the bar.

Jamie fingered the empty whiskey glass and turned toward the mirror behind the bar. Glancing at his reflection, he admired his smooth facial features—not bad for a thirty-six-year-old guy. *How old might the lady be?* he wondered. Perhaps younger by a couple of years, judging from her firm and desirable body. *Hey, wait a minute,* his brain said. *Are you lusting? No! You can't be,* his inner voice answered.

Was he being foolhardy? Should he be listening to his conscience rather than his common sense? Did he have an ulterior motive for wanting to protect this woman? Granted, she was beautiful, especially after he'd provided proper clothing and had Hattie fix her hair to hide the scarring on her face. She was stunning now. And how could he forget the electric spark that ran through his hand every time he touched her. As a professed bachelor in his mid-thirties, he wouldn't have ever thought he'd experience such feelings. Since becoming a barkeep, he'd acknowledged that marriage or any kind of attachment to the opposite sex wasn't in the cards. Few saloon owners and barmen married and had families. Jamie hadn't thought it much of a sacrifice. Working in a saloon wasn't as exhausting as working in the silver mines of Colorado or as dangerous as being a lawman in Arizona. He didn't even mind the fact that he'd given up the study of law to seek his fortune. He'd disappointed his family, but his adventurous spirit held more sway with him than family ties. Money and a future was what he sought, if only his conscience would allow. The opportunity for owning his own saloon in Idaho intrigued him more than Alaska gold mining, the only other option offering quick riches. Strangely, he felt this lady he'd saved was part of God's plan for achieving his life goals.

Jamie had done all he could to make his small two-room apartment above the bar comfortable. The floor was spotlessly clean, the chairs free of clutter, the blind rolled up to hide the ugly rip. He'd carried up Irish stew from the bar, along with a day-old loaf of sourdough bread for their dinner. He'd set the table carefully with the mismatched plates, silverware, and even napkins brought from the kitchen below. He'd pulled the shaky wooden table to a level spot in the middle of the room. He wanted tonight to be special for his lady because he wished to discuss a delicate subject with her.

Putting down his fork, he said, "I'm thinking about leaving San Francisco to get away from all this chaos. Would you like to go with me?" He watched for her reaction, something he'd learned to do over the past few weeks. She wasn't much for words, but her face, especially her eyes, usually disclosed her responses to his words. Watching carefully, he read very little interest, if not total disinterest, in her expression. She moved the food around her plate, picking up a bite, setting it down, and then moving the bite to another spot on her plate. Jamie had observed his grandma do this as she aged but never a younger woman, except when one was nervous. He wondered what it signified. Perhaps insecurity?

He cut a slice of meat and added a large piece of potato on top before he dipped it in his gravy and put it in his mouth. Chewing slowly, he considered the next topic he had to discuss: a name for her. He couldn't keep referring to her as "my lady."

Looking up from his plate after cutting another bite, he said, "I think we need to come up with a name for you until you can remember your own name. How does that sound to you?" She shared a nod of agreement before she placed a dainty bite of potato in her mouth. "Well then, what would you like to be called? Do you have a preference?"

Gracefully dabbing the right side of her lip with her napkin and returning it to her lap, the woman across from Jamie gazed at him. She answered softly, "Something beginning with E would be nice."

Thunderstruck at her immediate response, Jamie stopped chewing, put down his fork, pushed back his chair, and crossed his right leg over his left knee. He'd received an answer from her! The face across from him appeared untroubled, pleased to have answered his question, and, yes, almost grateful that he'd broached the subject. Why hadn't he asked this question weeks ago? Of course she'd want to be called by a name, rather than "my lady." He'd introduced himself by name immediately after she'd recovered from the shock of being rescued. *How stupid and thoughtless of me.*

"A lady's name beginning with an E it is, then. How about Eve, from the first book in the Bible? Or another biblical name like Esther, or, perhaps Estelle?"

The last brought an adamant headshake and a giggle

from across the table. He grinned; it was the first time she'd smiled in his presence. "Well then, there's Elisha, Esmeralda, Eunice or Ellie?" Each resulted in a fervent no response. Jamie continued. "Emily? Emma? How about Elizabeth then? If you like, we could shorten it to Liz?" At the last name mentioned, he saw a faint smile spread across her face. Winking in agreement, Jamie uncrossed his leg and straightened in his chair. "Elizabeth or Liz it is, then."

As they approached the gangplank of the *Maryjane*, which would transport them to Seattle, heat shot up Jamie's arm when Liz grasped it. With trepidation, he centered his other hand on her arm to steady her as they stepped further up on the gangplank. Reaching the deck, she continued holding fast to his arm. He heard a soft chuckle behind him that sent prickles of heat up the back of his neck. *Darn that Dillon*, he thought.

Onboard, Jamie looked around for someone to give them directions, but everyone was busy stowing away crates in the open hold, so they were on their own. Spotting a door ahead, Jamie guided Liz forward, helping her to step around puddles of water on the deck. The door led into a short hallway with a stairway off to one side leading downward. "I'll bet this will take us down to our cabin," Jamie stated, leading the way. Suddenly their noses tickled and twitched at the overwhelming scent of cedar.

The cabin assigned was small, about five feet by eight; the bunk bed took up most of the space. The bunk's mattress was held in place by a lip that also prevented the occupant from tumbling out. There was enough room for one person walking sideways to pass between the bed and wall. Above the bunk was a porthole. Sizing up the bed's length, Jamie realized neither he nor Dillon could stretch out in the bunk, but it would work perfectly for Liz because she was so short, barely reaching his chin. Under the bed was storage space. A low stool stood between the bed and the bulkhead for climbing into the bunk. Three wooden pegs on one wall would do for hanging clothing.

Liz frowned upon entering the cabin. Turning to Jamie, who stood in the doorway, she asked, "Will we all fit in here?"

"No, this cabin is just for you. Dillon and I will be sleeping topside, on the deck."

"But a whole family could use this space. When I sailed before, our entire family didn't have even this much space in the hold."

Shifting his feet, Jamie looked with interest at Elizabeth. Was she beginning to recover some of her memory? Up to now she'd been a blank slate, not remembering anything and not saying much. Now she remembered being on a ship before. Perhaps this was the beginning of a breakthrough. "You've sailed before?"

"No," answered Liz, looked at him with a frown. "I don't think so, but the sway underneath me seems vaguely familiar. Have we sailed somewhere before?"

"No. This is our first time sailing together," answered Jamie, cutting off his speech before adding the word *sweet-ums* to his reply. He stepped carefully into the cabin and stowed their belongings under the bed. He and Dillon would retrieve their sleeping bags later.

"Want to go topside and watch our departure from the harbor?"

Liz went first as they headed toward the ladder leading to the deck. Jamie followed, thinking about her comment about sailing before. The sway of the ship didn't appear to impeded her steps. She adjusted to the ship's movement, widening her usual mincing footsteps to steady herself. Following behind, not too closely, he ascended the ladder. He couldn't help notice her slim ankles and the used shoes he'd found for her in San Francisco. They were way too big for her. Why hadn't he noticed before? He remembered his own experience as a youngster, having to wear his brother's hand-me-down shoes that never fit, even with newsprint stuffed in them, which caused blisters. He promised himself that as soon as they reached Seattle he'd purchase her a pair that fit.

San Francisco Harbor was crowded with US naval ships. Thankfully they'd been in port when the earthquake hit. Because all the municipal leaders were either injured or killed when the initial quake occurred, the navy took over running the city government and rescue efforts. Trained to go into action immediately, the sailors had saved many lives; they set up emergency hospital facilities and organized able-bodied civilians to help until additional military and civilian help could arrive. President Roosevelt immediately ordered all trains diverted to the West Coast to assist the devastated city. Medical supplies, food, housing in the form of tents, and trained personnel were rushed to the city. Even the closest army unit, days away in Los Angeles, marched day and night with their pack mules to reach the disaster area with needed supplies.

As Jamie, Dillon, and Elizabeth stood on deck waiting for the ship to leave the harbor, they saw only a few merchant ships like theirs tied up at the dock, waiting for permission from the navy to depart. Some cargo ships were lucky enough to sail prior to the earthquake, many bound for Japan. They were lucky the quake didn't cause a tidal wave to block them from the Pacific Ocean.

Jamie felt a weight lifted from him now that they were aboard and setting sail. He wanted to be away from all this devastation. The quake was one thing, but the aftermath and the fires jumping from building to building, block by block, was nightmarish. He hoped he'd never have to experience that again. Glancing at Liz beside him, he couldn't help but thank God that he'd been in the right place at the right time to save her.

Chapter 3

• • • • • • •

Sailing North

Jamie leaned over the deck railing, watching as the ship sailed northward through the open waters of the Pacific Ocean. This was his first ocean trip. He welcomed the smoothness under his feet compared to when they'd left San Francisco Bay and entered the rough open waters that brought on Liz's onslaught of seasickness. She was abed in the cabin and had been for the past few days. Earlier he'd taken a mug of weak tea and a biscuit to her, but she still couldn't bear to face any nourishment.

He and Dillon, seasoned travelers, had only experienced slight twinges as the ship rolled and heaved out of San Francisco Bay. Jamie admitted to himself but not to his friend that he'd swallowed his breakfast twice rather than embarrass himself by throwing up. He felt sorry for Liz, who suffered her first episode of seasickness in front of them.

Feeling someone approach, Jamie glanced up to see Dillon's swaying form and silently greeted him with a nod. The two friends stood, each with one hand on the ship's railing, facing each other.

"How's Liz doing this morning?" inquired Dillon.

"You've accepted her nickname. I approve," nodded Jamie. "She's still in her bunk and can't look at food without barfing. I wish I could get her topside. The roll of the ship here isn't as bad as in the cabin."

"Too bad the cabin is so far forward. It takes the brunt of breaking through the waves for the whole ship," remarked Dillon. "But it's better than being aft."

"I know, but we're fortunate that there was a vacant cabin. Most of these small merchant ships going between San Francisco and Seattle don't take many passengers. They're mostly for hauling goods up and down the coast."

"I know, I know. But I sure wish we didn't have to sleep out in the open. Although the coiled rope isn't as bad as I imagined, the cold seeps into my bones by morning. Thank goodness I'm young enough and don't have arthritis like my mom. I'd be in a bad way if I did," commented Dillon, rubbing his left arm with his hand. "Tonight, I plan to pull out my long johns, my heavy jacket, and my woolen knit cap. My one blanket isn't enough to keep the chill away."

"I know what you mean," came the reply beside him. Glancing upward, Jamie wished the small wooden roof above gave them more cover from the elements, but it had been constructed to shield only the doorway. "Even though it's the end of May, it's cold out here in the open sea air. I wonder how the men going up to Alaska manage. I heard the captain say that most of the passengers heading north sleep on the decks because the cost of cabins is so high. He said the lucky ones know enough to bring tents."

"Maybe that's what we should have done," moaned Dillon, stomping his feet.

Jamie chuckled, visualizing them trying to set up a tent on a deck, let alone keeping it from blowing away in the wind at night. "Yaw, but we'd never have gotten out of San Francisco with a tent. They're all being used to shelter earthquake survivors," Jamie said, pulling his knit cap farther down on his head. The wind had picked up and blew saltwater on them.

Wiping spray from his face, Dillon motioned for them to move away from the railing. Leaning inward, he stroked his jaw, which was still raw from a rope burn the first night sleeping aboard. Silence descended between the two friends, both deep in their own thoughts. A passing Chinese sailor grinned at them as he gave a slight bow. The crew was mostly Scandinavian, except for a couple of Chinese boys and the cook.

The first night aboard Jamie had sat down to the first meal he hadn't prepared for himself in a long time. Platters of roast beef and vegetables were passed around to a crew so hungry that not a word was spoken for a good ten minutes. His hunger soothed, Jamie looked around the table and wondered where the crew were from but was wise enough not to ask. Finally, as each shoved their empty plate into the center of the table, they leaned back in their chairs and smiled contentedly. Taking the cue from their body language, Jamie asked," Where's home for you all?"

"Seattle, but actually a place called Ballard, a settlement close to Seattle."

"Never heard of it, "replied Jamie, pushing his chair back from the table to ease a cramp in one leg.

The first mate motioned toward Jamie with his mug before setting it down and asked in a snide tone, "Where's your lady friend traveling with you?"

"My lady friend, as you call her, is my sister Elizabeth," answered Jamie. "Unfortunately she's suffering with seasickness."

"Okay, be civil," interrupted the captain. "I hear you were in San Francisco during the earthquake. Was it as bad as reported? We sailed into the harbor a couple of hours after the first big shake. Didn't feel or notice a thing until the navy came aboard and gave us orders to drop anchor out in the middle of the bay and stay put."

"The worst part wasn't the quake itself," answered Jamie, "but the fires that erupted afterward. There wasn't water enough to fight them or enough manpower." Pausing, while crossing his legs, "I assume you were bringing in supplies?"

"No, that's the funny part of our story. We brought in a load of cedar shakes from Ballard, the shake capital of the world. Nothing the people of San Francisco needed at the moment."

Dillon nodded. "You're right. The city needed medical supplies, tents, and especially able-bodied men willing to dig through the rubble for survivors."

"What were you doing during the earthquake?" ask a sailor with a Norwegian brogue.

Jamie solemnly turned to the bearded sailor. "I was tending bar at the time. Everything shook, glasses and bottles toppled over crashing to the floor, breaking. I was petrified! Paralyzed! It was my first experience -," he choked as he stopped speaking.

His statement silenced the conversation around the table. Getting up from his chair, the captain announced, "Back to work," as he cleared his throat.

Jamie stood and nodded to the captain. "Excuse me. I think I should see if Liz is feeling well enough to try a biscuit and a spot of weak tea." Ducking through the door, he left the mess, where the crew ate at various times. A smiling and bowing cook's boy held a mug toward him and a napkin. "Thank you," mouthed Jamie. He turned down the passageway toward the cabin. A sudden turbulence unbalanced him, sending him sideways. "Damn," escaped from his lips as hot tea spilled on his fingers. He used the napkin to carefully wipe his smarting hand. Leaning a shoulder against the wall to steady himself, he continued slowly down the passageway.

Knocking on the cabin door, Jamie waited for an answer. Hearing only a groan, he entered cautiously. Liz lay curled in the bunk, not looking much better than she had in the morning. She appeared wan and pale-faced as she clutched the bed cover. "I brought you some tea and a biscuit." She didn't turn away from him, so Jamie helped lift her onto one elbow. He handed her the mug of tea. "This will get you back on your feet."

Jamie watched her drink the tea and pick at the biscuit, satisfied that she was probably over the worst of the seasickness. He said good-bye and returned the mug to the galley before finding his way to his coil of rope on deck and hopefully a night's sleep. Dillon, already curled up on his rope, thrashed about, attempting to find a comfortable position, as Jamie threw his dry rug over the mound of rope and lay down. "Sleep tight—don't let the rats get you," Jamie teased.

"Tie yourself in so you don't wash overboard," came the reply.

Chapter 4

• • • • • • •

Panic Attack

A sudden squall hit the *Maryjane*, sending saltwater over the ship's deck where the two men slept. Jamie and Dillon awoke with a start, completely soaked. Wiping the wetness from their faces, they jumped up, almost bumping into sailors still pulling on their slickers as they ran past. The first mate rushed past, shouting, "Get below! Stay off the deck!"

Struggling to stand upright, Jamie and Dillon swayed like inebriated sailors returning from shore leave as they slowly struggled against the rocking of the ship and headed toward the companionway leading below deck. Almost stepping on each other as they descended the ladder, their passage was abruptly halted by Liz who was climbing up.

"Yikes! Liz, stop. Go back. We're coming down," yelled Jamie.

"No, no, let me out," wailed Liz, shoving one of Jamie's feet off the ladder. Liz struggled forcefully, butting her head, her arms pushing and tugging, trying to eject Jamie from above her. "Let me up!" she screamed hysterically, lifting Jamie's legs one by one from the ladder.

Gripping the rungs with his hands, Jamie swung out over Liz to land on his feet. Reaching out, he grasped Liz's waist and pulled her from the ladder, allowing Dillon to complete his descent. She continued to thrash and kick, making him almost lose his already unsteady balance as the ship rolled. She screamed into his ear words he'd never heard before and couldn't understand; they sounded foreign. Liz was strong. He had his hands full just holding onto her. "Stop it, Liz," he shouted over her tirade. "It's just a storm we have to ride out. Stop struggling. Let's get back to your cabin. Dillon and I will stay with you. You'll be safe."

Liz continued to tussle, attempting to free herself from the arms holding her. She hammered his chest and kicked his ankles. Walking her to the cabin was impossible.

Standing by, helplessly watching his friend being pummeled by a slip of a ranting woman half his size, Dillon muttered through his teeth, "I suggest picking her up and carrying her to the cabin before she overpowers you. Of course, if you can't handle the spitfire there, I could help you."

Giving Dillon a dirty look, Jamie placed one arm under Liz's legs and the other arm tightly around her waist. He hoisted the squirming figure up into his arms. Walking from side to side with the roll of the ship and using the companionway walls to maintain his balance, he slowly made his way to her cabin. He dumped the panicked woman onto the bunk bed. At once she attempted to climb out, pushing and shoving, trying to escape. The lurching ship tossed her back into her bunk rather than tossing her out. More unrecognizable words were uttered. Exasperated, Liz gave up thrashing about and began sobbing.

Jamie and Dillon looked at each other. As the ship rolled from side to side, pitching up and down, the two found standing difficult. Finally, Dillon, knees bent, slid down the closed cabin door onto his rear.

Jamie chuckled. He looked around the small floor space and wondered where he might sit. Just then Liz flung her legs over the side of the bunk and launched herself out of the bed. With Dillon blocking the door, Jamie reached out and grabbed the minx around the waist. "No, you don't. Ugh!" he said, collapsing on the floor with Liz from an elbow to his stomach. He felt slightly dizzy as he fought for breath.

Gripping Liz firmly around the waist and throwing one leg across her thrashing legs, he attempted to quiet her movements enough so neither of them were injured as the vessel rocked. They heard the loud clanking of the anchor against the ship's side. Waves washed against the porthole, obliterating the view. The ship creaked. In places beads of water seeped between the wooden wallboards. Jamie began to pray for their safety. He'd heard of too many shipwrecks in storms like this with all lives lost. This was not the way he planned to end his thirty-five-years of existence. He'd not made his fortune yet. Yes, he wanted to be rich and a pillar of the community. Damn that San Francisco earthquake! It broke his lucky streak.

To protect his chest from Liz's headbutting, he rested his chin on the top of her head. As she went limp, he relaxed. Eventually sleep overtook them both.

The saloon where he'd found work in San Francisco

had been a gold mine. It stayed open day and night, filled with sailors and incoming travelers from the East, ready to drink and gamble, with their pockets full of money. Jamie was a good bartender, affable and outgoing, with a wide variety of stories to share with his clients. The owner of the saloon found him trustworthy and honest, so he was given a lot of latitude in running the saloon during the early morning hours. He was allowed to tend the bar, as well as gamble if he so desired. That's how it came about that one evening when he joined a group of men playing high stakes poker, Jamie won big. Smiling, he began his favorite activity: dreaming of a fabulously furnished Victorian house on acres of green fields dotted with horses. He would ride through fields each day, enjoying his blessings of wealth. A smile crept across his face, and his body relaxed as his mount cantered over the lush fields.

Jamie awoke abruptly. He couldn't feel his horse under him, just a weight pushing down on him. Where was he? Opening one eye, he saw strands of yellow hair spread out upon his chest. Over his torso lay a small female body. His right arm, which held his charge firmly in place, was now sending him urgent throbbing messages.

Jamie no longer felt the ship pitching violently; it moved smoothly, almost motionless. Looking toward Dillon, still slumped across the door, he saw amusement register on his friend's face. Self-consciously, Jamie gently extracted his right arm from around Liz. Turning and twisting the numb arm, he tried to regain some feeling. Liz moved toward his right side, snuggling deeper into his firm, muscular body. She grasped an area close to his right underarm to maintain balance. Now Jamie had to be content to leave his right arm curled around his own neck if he didn't want to awaken her.

Looking across at Dillon, who wore a lopsided, toothy grin, Jamie recognized he was being teased about his very intimate position with Liz. He answered with a frown and shook his head as vigorously as he could without awakening Liz, sprawled on top of him. A knock on the door interrupted their silent exchange.

"Are you guys okay in there? The storm's passed. It's safe for you to come out."

"Yes, we're fine," Jamie answered, watching as Dillon pushed himself up the door and onto his feet. Liz's languid eyes opened. Her expression turned to mortification as she realized that she was cradled in Jamie's arms. Hurriedly she pushed herself away, mindful of where she placed her hands. She felt his muscular frame tighten as he steadied her with one hand as she slid sideways. The two used each other and the wall for balance as they maneuvered to stand up. Embarrassed, Liz straightened her dress, keeping her eyes lowered as Jamie tucked his shirttail into his pants. Turning toward to the door, he gestured to Dillon to open it. As the men left the cabin Jamie called, "Come up when you're ready."

On the deck, the two friends gingerly walked the slippery surface. Some of the crew were already starting to clean up from the storm. "I hope we don't have to experience many storms like that again. You couldn't offer me enough money to make sailing my career," commented Jamie.

"I thought you weathered that storm rather well," remarked Dillon as a sly smile crept across his face.

Jamie held his tongue, knowing that any retort

would only mean more jabs at the position he'd found himself in during the storm. Walking away from his friend, he considered his situation. Why hadn't he just left the woman in San Francisco to fend for herself? She was nothing to him, certainly not his responsibility. He was a sucker for women in distress, as his sister kept telling him.

The ship glided over the satiny surface, leaving bubbly streamers in its wake. One moment there could be horrible turbulence and the next great calm. One moment you thought your life was threatened and the next all unrest disappeared. Jamie looked forward to the time when he could settle down to a calm existence. Hopefully Liz would soon get her memory back so he could return her to where she belonged. But what if she didn't have a family? What if she never regained her memory? Then what would he do? Stroking his chin that now sported rough bristles, Jamie felt weariness surge through his body.

The rustle of a skirt alerted him to Liz's approach. Words tumbled from her lips. "Thank you for your help during the storm. I don't know why I got so frightened. All I wanted to do was run and hide. I didn't even realize I was on a ship. The motion and all the crackling sounds frightened me. I'm sorry I fell asleep on you. Will you forgive me? I'm really a very nice lady. I don't know what got into me. Please forgive my being so forward."

Jamie turned toward Liz, who fidgeted beside him, twisting something that wasn't there around the ring finger of her left hand. He'd notice her doing this before, especially when she became confused. Often when she sat, she held her left hand with her right and rubbed the ring finger as if something were missing. Smiling down at her now, he forgot all his worries about their situation. He felt protective of her. "Don't worry about what happened during the storm. We were all frightened. I'm just glad we were together."

Chapter 5

Seattle, Washington

After arriving in Seattle, Jamie and Dillon disembarked. They both laughed as they stepped onto the wharf but continued feeling the sway of the ship as they walked. They went in search of lodgings. The captain had warned them that with the Alaskan gold rush, housing was scarce. As they hiked toward the main business center, Jamie commented, "Doesn't look as prosperous as San Francisco before the quake, does it?"

"Yeah, rather more like a frontier town," answered Dillon. "Growing but not attracting wealthy investors."

"Well, it's a seaport like San Francisco. It's just not attracting enough of the Asian trade as Tacoma. I hear its harbor is better equipped to facilitate overseas commerce than here."

"Yes, but Seattle has the Alaska market," returned Dillon.

"How about you take one side of the street and I'll take the other," Jamie suggested. "Let's go a couple of blocks. Remember, we need rooms as well as jobs. My purse is nearly empty."

At noon, the two friends met at the Central Saloon on First Avenue to compare progress. Between them they'd covered most of the waterfront. Over their favorite beverage, the two talked about widening their search. Fortunately, they did have another day before having to leave the *Maryjane*. For a small fee the captain had agreed they could remain aboard an extra night while the crew took on cargo before heading back to San Francisco.

As the two discussed their problem, the barman interrupted. "Did I overhear correctly that you're looking for work as well as lodging?"

"Yep, that's correct."

"So you're not bitten by the 'gold bug' and plan to remain in Seattle?"

Sliding his now-empty milk glass toward the chatty barman, Jamie nodded. "Yep, we really need jobs. Cost us a bundle to get away from the chaos down in San Francisco."

"Bet that was some show down there. We went through almost the same here in 1889—not an earthquake, mind you, but fire. Started right here on First and Madison and spreading quickly through all of downtown. Thirty blocks of businesses gone. People thought Seattle was a goner as a city. Many assumed that besides San Francisco, Tacoma would become the leading seaport on the West Coast. We learned our lesson, however; no more wooden buildings, just bricks and stone." Chuckling, he wiped the bar in front of Jamie. "We export our logs down to San Francisco and across the Pacific to Japan. We ship a lot of shingles all over the world too. Our forests are a gold mine."

"Sounds like Seattle has solved all its problems," remarked Dillon.

"Not entirely. Problems remain with these darn hills around here. Politicians are dragging their feet over leveling them. Then there's the need for a better water supply. Anyway, you looking for work?"

"He is," answered Dillon, pointing toward his friend."

"Well, if you don't mind walking, I know Merchant's on Yesler Way is looking for a barman. I've heard that they often have rooms for their employees. Worth checking out."

❄

"Slow up. I can't keep up with you."

Jamie stopped, forgetting Liz had a hard time keeping up with her minuscule steps and oversized shoes. Dillon was striding ahead and probably hadn't heard Liz's cry to slow down. Waiting for her, Jamie contemplated their good luck. If they hadn't stopped at the Central Saloon; if the barkeep there hadn't been forthcoming with the information about the job at Merchant—if, if—they'd be stranded now. Yes, what good fortune! Even Dillon took a job at Merchant's, earning them two rooms rather than one. Thank goodness Dillon was willing to forget his oath to never take a chef's job ever again, even if he had to starve.

Dillon grew up on an Idaho dryland farm and escaped just as soon as the opportunity arose. First, he'd tried mining north of Boise City. When the camp cook left, he'd been coerced into taking his place because of his youth. Cooking wasn't his thing until he began listening to suggestions from older miners. The job improved, but he grew tired of the monotony of stew pots, baking, and grilling. He craved change, as had Jamie, so the two had joined forces.

Merchant's, considered one of the best saloons in the city, as well as a respectable café, had been in business since 1890. Jamie cringed when he thought of the lie he'd told to get the lodging for them. When asked about Liz, he'd identified her as his sister. He'd been alert enough not to say she was his wife. As a good Methodist, he knew he shouldn't tell untruths. Perhaps just this once God would forgive him, especially since he was caring for her until her memory returned. He should be rewarded for his good deed, shouldn't he? What was it the Lutherans say, 'Adding a star to your crown'?

One room provided by Merchant's was adequate for Liz: single bed and a chair, with a couple of hooks on a wall for clothing. His and Dillon's room also had a single bed, but they worked different shifts so could make do with one bed, a common practice, especially with men who worked different stints. Everyone shared the one bathroom at the end of the hall. The job gave him and Dillon their meals; the price for Liz's food was only five or ten cents per day. Jamie reasoned that with Dillon in the kitchen there wouldn't be any problem saving her leftovers. "We'll make it work," Jamie and Dillon both agreed.

When he took the job, Jamie gave no thought to what Liz might do while they worked. Actually, he'd never considered what women did with their time until Dillon asked him, "What do you plan to do with Liz during the day? She's not going to want to stay cooped up all the time."

For the first couple of days at Merchant's, the problem of Liz's unoccupied time solved itself. She slept after downing a cup of coffee Dillon brought her in the morning. In the evenings after his shift, he sat with her in her room, talking about problems he confronted in the kitchen while she ate the plate of leftovers he brought her. Jamie was already on his stint at the bar. On the third day, around noon Liz found her way to the kitchen. Dillon looked up from the stove as she entered. "Welcome. Hungry?"

She gave him a big smile and nodded. "Jamie told me where to find you as he headed to the bathroom. I thought I'd come find you."

Motioning toward a tiny table, Dillon smiled. "Have a seat and I'll fix you something." As Liz glanced around the sparkling clean kitchen, he threw some meat on the grill, along with potato slices. Soon a plate full of food appeared in front of her, along with a mug of hot coffee. "There you are—enjoy. Want some catsup?" Liz, who had already taken in a forkful of potato, shook her head.

Dillon soon got busy with orders, forgetting about Liz until he heard water splash and dishes clink. Turning toward the sink area, he saw Liz's bare-arms deep in soapy water as she washed dirty glasses, mugs, and plates. She'd rolled up her sleeves and tied a towel around her waist, her face placid, intent on the job. Pleased to have the help, Dillon began to whistle. Pretty soon Liz began to hum along with him.

"What have we here?" Jamie asked, entering the kitchen. "I could hear you singing out in the bar."

"Just happy workers," announced Dillon. "I've a volunteer dishwasher."

Smiling at Liz, Jamie asked, "Bored without us?"

As days passed, Jamie was delighted that Liz began to accompany Dillon to the kitchen in the mornings rather than remaining in bed. After a brief breakfast, she set about helping Dillon with whatever food preparation was necessary until the dirty dishes piled up. She then rolled up her sleeves and set to work. Soon the manager discovered Liz working in the kitchen. She was offered free meals in exchange for her help.

To encourage her to become more social, Jamie suggest she accompany Dillon to the bar one night when there was a special vaudeville group performing. The two dressed up. Liz donned her new long black gathered skirt and white long-sleeved blouse. Dillon wore a clean pair of faded blue trousers and button-down striped shirt. They found a table with two of Jamie's friends. The place was noisy, crowded, and smelly. As the time for the performance drew near, Mr. Lewis, owner of the bar, appeared on the stage, announcing that the pianist hadn't shown up. The night's performance was cancelled.

Boos and two-fingered whistles erupted. People began to bang their mugs on the tables. Loud shouts from the audience calling for the show to go on sounded. Just as Dillon was about to turn to Liz to suggest they leave, notes coming from the piano filled the air. All eyes centered on Mr. Lewis as he returned to the stage. Raising his hands, he announced that a substitute pianist had been found. The show would go on.

Dillon turned toward Liz to share the news with her. She wasn't beside him. Looking around, he couldn't spot her. Where was she? Standing up, he searched for Jamie, who motioned with his head toward the piano. There sat Liz!

❧

After that eventful evening, their savings increased quickly. Jamie confessed one evening, "I can't continue carrying all our money around my neck," dangling the fist-size pouch in front of them. It was obvious something had to be done. "I've rigged it so it goes under my arm, but the pouch is still too large. Some stranger coming into the bar is going to figure out what the bulge under my arm is and rob me."

"Well, it's not safe to leave money in either of our rooms. There's no locks on the doors," said Dillon. "Even when we're sleeping it's not safe. We're so tired we'd never hear a soul enter or leave."

"I could hide it under my skirts."

"Yes, and if someone mauled you they'd know right away what you were hiding. No, we have to figure out something else."

After much discussion among the three friends, they agreed to divide the money. That way if one got robbed they wouldn't lose all their funds. Jamie devised a new flat leather pouch to go under his arm. Dillon created false insoles for his shoes to hide the money. Liz sewed several pockets into her petticoats to hold her money.

Now that Jamie and Dillon knew of Liz's musical talent, it was decided that they should take advantage of the wealth of cultural events in Seattle. Both hoped that the familiar musical environment might trigger her memory. Thus it was that the two men began escorting Liz during off hours to various musical events.

The Ladies Musical Club begun around 1891, gave monthly concerts. At the first concert Liz attended she heard Teresa Carreno, a Venezuelan child prodigy, considered the world's most famous woman pianist. After hearing her play, Liz couldn't stop talking about her technique. Dillon listened carefully, waiting for an appropriate moment to question her. "You know a lot about piano playing. Where did you get your training?"

"I received my training with Professor—" Liz stopped, looking blank. She appeared to be searching for a name but couldn't come up with it. Shaking her head, she brought her hands up to her head. "Why can't I remember?"

Putting his arm around her, Dillon gave a gentle squeeze. "Don't worry. It will all come back to you when you're ready."

"But when?"

"It's already starting. Look, you recalled being able to play the piano. It came to you very naturally. The rest will in time."

Smiling weakly up at him, she nodded. "Thank you for taking me to the concert. Teresa Carreno was superb. I've had the privilege of hearing two famous musicians."

"Oh? Who else have you heard?"

"Caruso, the Italian tenor."

"Oh, you heard him in San Francisco?" asked Dillon, looking down at the lovely lady walking beside him. Liz stopped walking at his question. He noticed she'd started twisting the imaginary ring on her left ring finger. Looking up at him with a blank face, she started off toward their destination without answering the question.

Chapter 6

• • • • • • •

August 1907
Seattle

Their year in Seattle slipped by quickly. Both Jamie and Dillon worked as many hours as allowed, intent on accumulating money to achieve their Idaho dreams. After Liz discovered her musical talent, she found herself in demand by other businesses, not just the saloon. She became a substitute pianist for a vaudeville group. The Grand Opera House hired her as a practice pianist, as did the Star and Orpheum theaters.

She visited Chinatown frequently, fascinated by the curio shops, drawn for some strange reason to Oriental carpets. As her musical career blossomed, she'd ceased helping Dillon in the kitchen; however, she did return from her wanderings in Chinatown with bundles of strange spices and vegetables with which he experimented. She shared with Jamie descriptions of what she saw and who she met.

In Seattle it was common to hear Italian, Greek, Japanese, and German spoken on the streets. To her surprise, Liz discovered that she understood as well as spoke German. Excitedly she'd told Jamie of her discovery. He encouraged her to visit the shops where she'd heard German. "Perhaps it will jog your memory."

She became a regular visitor to many of the shops run by the immigrant German Jews. It wasn't long before she was asked to help at the Settlement House on Twelfth and Washington Street, opened to aid the many Russian and Polish Jewish families displaced from their homeland by pogroms. Liz took on the job of teaching the children English, using music and songs to introduce words. Soon she organized a children's choir, along with a few students taking piano lessons. Liz blossomed with all these activities, especially those with the children.

Seattle city law closed the saloons on Sundays, enabling Jamie and Liz to spent the day together. Dillon worked all day in the café serving special Sunday meals and couldn't join them.

The horseless carriage was still a novelty in the Northwest. Many people still relied on horses and carriages to travel any distance. At the beginning of the century private trains ran into Seattle from newly developed housing areas, an idea the contractors came up with to entice buyers from the city center out into the surrounding areas. Later these small trains came under the ownership and management of the Seattle Electric Company, which held the franchise for the all the streetcars.

Although the streetcars service was erratic, Jamie and Liz took advantage of the cheap transportation. One of the first places Jamie wished to see was the newly opened campus of the University of Washington. The one-building institution had moved in 1894 from downtown out to its new location on Lake Washington near Union Bay. Mostly surrounded by old-growth trees and native plants, it was an ideal place to imagine what the countryside had looked like while the native Indian population inhabited the area before the coming of the white man.

Jamie loved sports, especially football. By 1889 American public universities became interested in promoting the sport; some even began hiring trainers from Europe; most were former boxers. On the West Coast, the University of Washington was one of the leaders in starting a football program. By 1907 the college was actively searching for a professional coach who could bring notoriety to the college. Football was unfamiliar to Liz. She and Jamie attended as many games as they could, but until Jamie began to explain the game, she saw it only as a group of strangely dressed boys throwing an oddly shaped ball around.

One of their Sunday outings took them to Madison Park. Once a private enterprise, it was now owned by the city. "Shall we walk along the beach first?" Jamie asked as they got off the streetcar.

Looking around, Liz smiled at all the couples holding hands as they strolled the beach. Slowly she moved her hand over toward Jamie's and slipped it into his. He made no move to remove his hand, and like the other couples, they strolled the beach hand in hand.

"Have you ever been canoeing?" he asked, noticing several couples on the water.

"No, I don't think so, but I've been in a small boat on a river."

"Where was that?"

A blank look crossed Liz's face. "I don't know. I don't know why I even said that."

Jamie glanced at his companion and knew immediately she'd remembered something and lost it as soon as she'd voiced it. "Don't worry about it. It doesn't matter." They walked on in silence until he spotted a space where they could sit. Taking off his jacket, he spread it on the ground. "Let's sit a while. Shall we?"

The sunny balmy weather was a pleasant change from the last several days of fog and dampness. On arrival in Seattle, the three friends hadn't minded the cooler and often rainy weather, but as the months dragged on, they all began to crave the sunshine they'd left behind in California. Liz found that during long periods of rain, she spent more time with her German friends. They'd taught her how to knit as they sat chatting, enjoying the beer that Jamie donated for her to share. Somehow carrying that pail of beer seemed vaguely familiar, but she didn't know why. She soon discovered that knitting kept her fingers nimble for piano playing at the saloon. It was a powerful revelation.

Late in August, while Jamie, Dillon, and Liz were enjoying one of their few suppers together, Jamie announced, "How about getting out of this damp and rainy city? I think we've enough money to make our trip to Idaho. We can leave next week if we like."

Liz clapped her hands as she looked from one man to the other.

Dillon silently stared at Jamie.

After they returned to the room they shared, he confronted Jamie. "Have you lost all reason? You can't take Liz to Idaho with you. Leave her here with her Jewish German friends. Let them care of her."

Facing his friend, Jamie spat out, "She goes with me. She's no concern of yours." Turning, he began to get ready to go to the bar for his shift. Under his breath, he said, "She's made some real progress here in Seattle, but she's still a long way from full recovery. She still doesn't know who she is. I'm not going to chance a relapse. That could very well happen if I abandon her now. No, she goes with me."

Banging his fist on the door frame through which Jamie was about to exit, Dillon shouted, "Then you go alone! I don't want to be any part of kidnapping, and that's what it is. Wake up, Jamie, before it's too late. What you're doing is wrong."

A knock startled the pair. Opening the door, Jamie faced Liz. She stepped into the room and closed the door behind her. "I couldn't help overhearing what you two were shouting." Looking from one to the other, she turned to Jamie. "I'm not anybody's responsibility, certainly not yours. I can make my own decisions, thank you. I appreciate all that you've done for me." Drawing a breath, she turned toward the door. Before walking out, she turned back. "I won't be going to Idaho with you, Jamie."

Jamie's shoulders fell. He turned toward Dillon. "Now see what you've done."

For several days, only necessary conversation was exchanged between the three. Silence reigned. Each went about their daily routines without smiles. On the third day, late in the afternoon, Jamie was behind the bar when three stocky dock workers walked up to the bar. Jamie glanced at them. Their faces looked familiar, but they weren't regulars and he couldn't place them.

"What'll it be?"

"You the one who has been sending beer over to our wives with Liz?" asked the tallest of the three.

Jamie peered from one to the other. Recognition dawned. These were the husbands of Liz's German women friends. "Yes," he gulped.

"We hear you plan to head for Idaho soon and leave her here. Is that true?"

Sucking in his breath, Jamie straightened to his full six feet before answering. "That's what she wants." His eyes darted among the three men in front of him.

"I'm Jacob," the younger man wearing a black cotton cap said. "My wife, Helga, tells me your Liz is all broken up about you leaving her. She claims you and your friend are abandoning her."

Jamie inhaled as he faced the three solidly built men in front of him. He realized any one of them could knock him flat with a punch. But three ...

"What kind of man are you to abandon a woman, and such a gifted person too? She thinks the world of you. Are you heartless?" asked the tallest.

"I'm Helene's husband, Fred," said the third man. "I've told my wife that Liz may room with us until she remembers who she is. So, you go on about your business in Idaho. We'll take good care of her." At that, the three men turned and left the saloon.

Jamie stood there, dazed. If he'd been a drinking man he would have poured himself a whiskey, but he'd sworn off booze long ago. He'd seen it wreck too many lives.

The kitchen door swung open. Dillon stood there, cleaver in hand. "I was ready if you'd needed me."

Jamie laughed and then hooted. "It was only three angry husbands of Liz's friends telling me what a fool I am for not taking her with me."

Dillon lowered his weapon. As he crossed to where his

friend stood, he snickered. "I heard it all," he confessed. "Now all you have to decide is if you want to follow your heart or that devilish logical mind of yours. Don't listen to me."

Chapter 7

• • • • • • •

Departing Seattle
August 1907

Jamie discovered that traveling to Idaho was easier said than done. All trains bypassed Boise City, the fastest-growing town in the territory. Eastern entrepreneurs who financed cross-country trains reasoned that seaports such as Seattle, Tacoma, Portland, and San Francisco weren't important enough commerce centers to require direct train connections to the eastern seaboard. Even the Alaskan gold rush didn't entice the tycoons into investing in tracks running through important cities like Boise. The closest train connection was to Kuna, Idaho, fourteen miles away. From there travelers had to rent horses or wagons to reach the gold fields north of Boise. It was possible to depart at Nampa and travel on a private branch line called the Stub that took riders into Boise City; it was primarily intended for carrying cargo and offered only one passenger car per trip.

    Jamie and Liz left from the recently built Seattle depot, counting themselves lucky that they hadn't had to travel to Tacoma to catch the westbound train. They sat together as the train climbed from the lush sea-level green of coastal Washington over the towering snow-capped Cascade Mountains into central Washington's rolling plains and hills. Whereas the coastal area they'd left was dotted by homesteads, houses, and buildings, the eastern plains they passed obviously lacked sufficient rain to remain green and were sparsely settled by occasional homesteads. Liz, content with her change of heart about traveling with Jamie to Idaho, sat knitting. She commented, "This central Washington scenery reminds me of the desert around my home."

Holding his breath, Jamie hoped she'd continue reminiscing about what desert she meant. "Mmm. This would be good cattle country. Look at the sagebrush. It looks just like ours at home," she observed. "But I don't see any piñon bushes. We burned piñon in our fireplaces. The smell's so wonderful. Have you ever smelled piñon?"

"No, I haven't," replied Jamie, turning in his seat to face her. He hoped the conversation would continue, but Liz lapsed into silence. He mulled over the information she'd shared. Now he knew she'd lived in a desert area somewhere. Her obsession with her ring finger indicated she was married or had been. She spoke German and was a gifted pianist. The pieces of her identify were being revealed. He just had to be patient. As the doctor in San Francisco had said, her memory would eventually return.

Liz's attention strayed to the family seated across from them. Next to the window, a young girl, intent on the passing scenery, held a cloth doll, recognizable as Raggedy Ann. Liz smiled as she watched the girl conversing softly with her doll. "Emma talked to her rag doll just like that," Liz commented, leaning forward at the waist for a better view. "She hardly spoke two words on our trip, except for imaginary conversations with Juanita." Suddenly stopping, Liz looked down at the knitting on her lap. "Why did I say that? Who could Emma be? What does she have to do with me?"

Jamie, giving her hand a squeeze, softly answered, "Don't worry about it. One of these days it will all come back."

"But more than a year has passed. I can't remember my name, my past, my family—anyone except you and Dillon. What if nothing comes back?"

"Amnesia is like that. Memories will come and go, according to the doctor. Now we're making new memories for us all. That's all that counts." Smiling, Jamie gave her hand a comforting pat.

After enjoying a lunch of sandwiches and apples washed down with cups of water, Jamie watched as Liz fought to stay awake. Soon her head fell forward, startling her upright. Jamie finally guided Liz's head onto his shoulder so she could nap.

Facing them was Dillon, his long legs constrained by the closeness of the seats and the other two pairs of legs. As Jamie tried to adjust his own cramped legs, he looked across at his friend; his thoughts drifted. What did the future hold for Dillon? His plan for going to Idaho was to farm, like his father before him. Also, he wanted to be closer to his sister, brother-in-law, nieces, and nephews. Jamie knew he'd worked hard to save enough money to be able to purchase land. Unlike Jamie, he wanted to settle down with a family. His brother-in-law, Doug, had suggested he look north near the Horseshoe Bend area, but that was too far away from his sister, Myra, so Dillon had selected Emmett as a likely spot. It was also close to Boise City, where he and Liz would settle.

Jamie saw Dillon's eyes flicker open to a slit as he began to survey the scene across from him. A broad smile crept across his whiskered face as he pulled his legs back. He winked at Jamie and closed his eyes.

Darn Dillon, thought Jamie, *he always reads desire into any kindness I show toward Liz,* even though he'd shown only brotherly kindness to her. Why couldn't Dillon see that? Shifting his gaze to the passing landscape, Jamie began to list in his head all he had to do after reaching Boise City.

Over the past several months, he'd been in touch with Walter E. Pierce, who operated one of the best real estate companies in Boise City. Meeting with him was a number one priority. In his last communication, Pierce wrote that he had several choice properties lined up for Jamie to consider. He'd already transferred his savings to the Pacific National Bank in Boise so that once he'd made a decision, a real estate deal could be handled expediently. The Pacific National Bank had been a practical choice since Walter Pierce served as a director of the bank. If a loan was needed, Pierce would certainly be amenable. Dillon had disregarded Jamie's advice to contact Pierce about land for sale around Emmett, saying he would rather rely on his brother-in-law. Dillon was leery of people he hadn't met, especially when it came to spending large sums of money.

Jamie felt a weight lift from his shoulder. Liz was awake. He gave her a smile. "Feeling rested?"

She nodded and straightened up, adjusting her skirt. "Did I sleep long? I hope you didn't mind my using your shoulder?"

He nodded. "Not in the least. In fact, I propped my head on yours so I could take a nap." The two smiled at each other self-consciously. A pinkish blush flashed across her cheeks. Liz lowered her eyes. Jamie scooped up the knitting that had fallen to the floor and placed it on her lap.

"Thank you."

Across from them a snicker erupted. Dillon crossed his legs and smiled broadly at the pair of them. "The two of you are quite something. How do you expect to pull off the story of being brother and sister in Boise City, acting the way you do? You won't fool a soul."

Angry, Jamie slapped his knee and rose. "I've got to stretch my legs."

As he walked up and down the aisle, he saw Liz return to her knitting. He admired her persistence once she'd decided on a goal. Before leaving Seattle, she'd insisted on purchasing enough wool for a sweater for each of them after she heard from her German friends that Boise City was cold. After choosing the wool, she'd started knitting immediately; she wanted to finish at least one sweater before their arrival in Boise. Jamie wondered if she had knit before she lost her memory. She'd taken to it so naturally. In his experience, most woman did knit, and cook, for that matter, something Liz was ill equipped to achieve except under Dillon's supervision. Coming back down the aisle toward his seat, he noticed Liz drop her knitting to her lap and stare out the window.

"A penny for your thoughts," Jamie interrupted, sliding in beside her after kneeing Dillon's sprawled torso.

Looking sideways, Liz smiled. "Did you stretch those long legs enough?"

"Yes, I think so. I met a man returning to Boise City

from Seattle. He's lived there since the 1880s. Appears we're moving to a progressive city. Although it has been isolated, with no direct railroad connection, it has a well-planned city street system, as well as roads to the surrounding area. He said we won't have any trouble getting around because the streets are well marked. The town's quite cosmopolitan, with a mixed ethnic population. There is a public library, an orphanage, theaters, and a symphony. They even have two newspapers, one Republican and the other Democrat. I don't think we'll miss Seattle."

"Sounds great! I should easily find work. That wasn't so in New Mexico," Liz commented.

"I didn't know you were familiar with New Mexico," remarked Jamie.

"I didn't know that either until just now," Liz said thoughtfully.

Jamie and Dillon exchanged looks. Here was another puzzle piece to her past. Had she been visiting San Francisco from New Mexico?

Liz didn't appear inclined to continue the conversation about New Mexico. Probably it was just another glimmer that passed through her mind and forgotten. They just had to be patient. Sooner or later all her disconnected thoughts would come together; then she'd remember her name and her past.

Jamie didn't stint on their accommodations in Boise City. He insisted they take rooms at the prestigious Idanha Hotel for four dollars per day. The hotel provided a well-stocked library off the lobby, as well as offering rental phones. Many leading citizens, like Governor Frank Gooding, resided there.

They were lucky they had advanced reservations at

the hotel because of the William "Big Bill" Haywood trial underway. The hotel was awash with attorneys, reporters, and the famous Clarence Darrow, representing Big Bill, charged in the murder of the former Idaho governor Frank Steunenberg, who tried to limit the unlawful practices of the Western Federation on Miners lead by Haywood.

Dillon stayed but one night in a two-dollar room before he headed for his sister's place in Emmett. For the first few days Jamie and Liz walked the streets, sightseeing. On one such walk they discovered the free Carnegie Library on Washington Street. While Jamie perused the two local newspapers, Liz found a novel to check out. In the evenings, they ate dinner at the lavish hotel dining room, after which Liz retired to her room to read. Jamie visited the hotel bar to rub shoulders with the town's night life. Although he was slightly younger than most of the businessmen who frequented the bar (he'd just turned forty), he got along well with the "older" clients, enjoying as much as they did the subject of local politics.

While Jamie began his search for a business property to invest in, a suite of rooms became available at the hotel, giving them a sitting room between two bedrooms. The arrangement proved much more convenient for both. Jamie had a rental piano brought in for Liz, and he now had a private place to discuss business with clients.

It wasn't long before Jamie was considering two properties, a saloon close to the train depot and a Victorian house on the edge of town on five acres. After purchasing both properties, Jamie set about planning a warehouse next to his saloon. Liz began the job of furnishing the house where they'd live as brother and sister. Her greatest joy was ordering a grand piano, as well as purchasing an older upright for use teaching piano.

While living at the hotel, Liz took on piano students in town, as well as others living on outlying ranches. Still very fit at thirty-nine, Liz enjoyed riding. To provide lessons to these rural students, she rented a horse from the nearby livery and rode to the ranches where the students lived. Liz left the operation of the smelly and onerous motorcar up to Jamie. Knowing her preference for horseflesh, Jamie went to farm auctions to look at horses to fill their barn. Life was taking shape for them both.

Chapter 8

• • • • • • •

Denver 1911

Arriving in Denver, Emma had only a faint recollection of when Caruso saw her off to travel down to Santa Fe when she was ten. She recalled how terribly frightened she'd been at being left so soon after the loss of her entire family in the San Francisco earthquake. Now here she was, a grown-up fifteen-year-old, again deserted by Papa. This time she was going after him rather than waiting for him to return to her. As she and Juan walked through the station, they marveled at the grandeur of the brick building and the smooth wooden seats for waiting passengers. Santa Fe's station was plain and rustic compared to this, she thought. Outside, they walked a short distance up the street to the Oxford Hotel. She'd heard it had reasonable rates that she could afford.

 The registration desk stood at the rear of a small but modestly furnished lobby. Opposite the stairs was a door leading into the dining room. Enticing food odors, especially freshly baked bread, drifted from the large space filled with tables where a number of people sat. Emma's taste buds puckered at the aroma.

The room she was shown was sparsely furnished but adequate: an iron single bed, straight chair, and a sink in the corner. The bathroom was down the hall. Juan rented a similar room on the floor above. It was the hotel's custom to rent unmarried single people arriving together, rooms on different floors.

Neither Juan nor Emma expected to remain in Denver, known as the Queen City, beyond a few days before they continued their travel westward. As they marked their third day waiting for a train, Emma became restless. She'd never had much patience, and she was in a hurry to reach Boise City to discover why Papa went there in such a hurry.

The reality of the cost of train tickets and living expenses surprised Emma. The money she'd thought would carry her to Idaho wouldn't. To Emma's chagrin, after two nights at the Oxford and paying for her meals, she and Juan had to economize by renting a room in a boardinghouse advertised "For Men Only."

"How do you expect us to manage?" asked Emma, looking quizzicality at the lumpy bed and one straight wooden chair. "I hope you don't expect me to sleep in the bed with you?"

"I could hope, couldn't I?" teased Juan, grinning, as he walked to look out the window. Turning back toward Emma, he threw his bedroll on the floor under the window. "I'll sleep here. You can have the bed."

A look of relief passed over Emma's face as she sat down on the edge of the double bed. "How do I manage the bathroom down the hall since only men live here."

Juan pulled the chair up, its back toward her, and

straddled the seat to face Emma. "Now, that *does* pose a problem, doesn't it, Gil?" He grinned with a sparkle in his eyes. "Especially if you want to take advantage of your one-bath-a-week privilege."

Emma reached out and playfully tried to slap at Juan. He dodged. "Be serious. It's a real problem."

"Wouldn't have it if you'd listened to all of us back home."

"Humph! We're here now. What are we going to do about our situation until we leave?"

Sensing that Emma had had enough teasing, Juan scratched his head. "Well, for one thing, since there's no lock on our bedroom door, I'm going to play Sir Cervantes and sleep against the door at night. I promise no 'tilting at adobe chimneys'." Grinning, he added, "Thank goodness there is a lock on the bathroom so I don't have to guard it while you're in there."

Staring at Juan, Emma tried to interpret his intentions. Was he sorry he'd joined her on the trip? Was he annoyed with her pretending to be a man? Or was he trying to solve their—no, her—problem? Did he blame her for not bringing sufficient funds for the trip? How she wished she could read his thoughts.

Juan visited the many saloons close to the hotel, looking for work. With his ranching experience, he was referred to one John Springer, an avid owner and breeder of thoroughbreds named Oldenburgs. These beautiful creatures from Germany, originally work animals pulling plows and wagons, were now coveted for riding because of their expressive heads, long legs, and size, typically sixteen to seventeen hands high (sixty-four to seventy inches). Springer owned many of these warmbloods, and as their breeder, he demanded expert care for them. Juan's college education in animal husbandry gained Springer's attention, despite the reality that he considered him a Mexican rather than Spanish. He was hired. Only after getting the job did he learn that his new boss was the same John Springer whose wife caused a bar fight that had left a man dead.

Denver in 1911 was abuzz about the Harold Frank Henwood trial. Henwood had shot and killed Von Phul and two other bystanders at the Brown Palace Hotel bar up the street from the Oxford. The fight between Henwood and Von Phul was over romantic letters Isabel Springer had written to Von Phul that Henwood, Isabel's other male friend, insisted be returned. The fracas at the hotel revealed to her husband, John Springer, her affair with Von Phul. It was the biggest scandal of upper-crust Denver society.

Emma walked the streets, grumbling to herself about what a fine fix they were in. She began to realize how limited jobs were for her as a smaller man. Thankfully, Juan had cautioned her to avoid any physically demanding jobs that would expose her lack of strength and thus her true identity. One day, she spotted a *Help Wanted* sign in the window of the Collier Mercantile Company. Because of the abundance of jobs available for men in Denver, perhaps the owner would consider a skinny, bookish-looking man for the job, she thought.

She entered the store and applied, expecting she'd be hired on the spot. But she left, discouraged, upon being told to come back tomorrow at six in the morning for an interview with the owner. The next day she arrived on time to find herself standing in a line with three burly men, all hoping to be hired. One by one, each was called into the office. Emma was the last to be interviewed. She was asked to lift a twenty-pound bag of flour. Next, she had to weigh out a pound of coffee. Last of all, Emma had to show how much yardage she would measure out for a dress and a man's shirt. With acumen, she complied with all three requests, reminding herself she must remember these questions once she returned to Santa Fe and interviewed people for jobs at their mercantile. They were excellent indicators of a person's skill. Emma got the job. Their financial situation was resolved for the moment.

Emma enjoyed her walk to work. Denver was so different from Santa Fe, with its paintings on the sides of buildings advertising products and businesses such as Becht Candies. The artists who created the ads, called "wall dogs," were quite talented. The sign painters worked with many mediums: wood, glass, metal, and brick. Unfortunately, the wall dogs often suffered from lead poisoning from the white paint they used.

Late one evening while walking home from work, Emma dodged her way around the many workers heading home after their nightly stop at a saloon. Most could handle their whiskey or beer, but a few couldn't. She watched as one drunk was led by a policeman to a small structure called a kiosk on a street corner and held there until transported to jail. The kiosks were so small, a man could only stand in them. Emma chuckled to herself; the kiosk kept the man upright so the police could easily handle him.

Emma found her clerking work tiring. She'd never realized how much of a load Wolfe had carried back in Santa Fe. Day after day she returned to the boarding house so exhausted that going down to supper required a lot of encouragement from Juan, who although also tired from work still had enough pep left to tease her into going to supper.

One evening she returned from work looking forward to her weekly bath. She decided to take it before supper. Grabbing her towel, washcloth, and soap, Emma took advantage of the vacant bathroom. Closing the door behind her, she undressed before sitting down on the john to wait for the tub to fill.

"For crying out loud!! You've flooded my kitchen. What a mess! Wake up, wake up. Look what you've done!" shouted a peevish voice in Emma's ear. She felt a hand shake her shoulder. Dazed, she straightened up and looked around. *Where am I? On no!* Quickly throwing her arms around her breasts, she looked into the knowing eyes of their landlady.

"Well, I never. You're a girl!" Mrs. Wallace slammed the bathroom door shut. Turning to Emma, she gave a humph as she threw her clothes at her. "Get dressed. You'll help clean up."

"Yes, ma'am." Still groggy and alarmed, Emma tugged on her clothing. Grabbing her towel, she began to wipe up the water around the tub.

"Use some of the dirty towels from the hamper there to finish the job. Afterward, come down to the kitchen. You'll help clean up there too." Facing Emma, Mrs. Wallace added, "Then you have some explaining to do, young lady."

As Emma grudgingly descended the stairs to the main floor, she wondered if she and Juan would find themselves evicted. Where would they go? She knew they still didn't have sufficient funds to travel to Idaho. Oh, why had she fallen asleep? What a mess she'd made of everything.

Hang-dog, she entered the kitchen to face Mrs. Wallace, who was busy wiping water off the drain boards adjacent to the sink. "Took your time. Go fetch the mop from the closet over there," she directed with the toss of her head. "Start wiping up the floors. I've got my hands full assembling another supper for everyone. The first one is ruined, but you wouldn't know about *that*, would you? Don't dawdle. I need your help."

Emma accepted the woman's jabs without complaining. She already felt bad enough over the trouble she'd caused. Facing Mrs. Wallace wasn't half as bad as explaining to Juan what she'd done was going to be. She wasn't looking forward to that at all.

After helping prepare supper, Emma and Mrs. Wallace talked. The landlady wasn't very understanding about her and Juan breaking the men-only house rule. Since they were paid up until the end of the week, she said, they could stay till then if Emma promised not to reveal her sex to the rest of the residents.

Getting through supper was hard. Juan sat across from her. He couldn't help notice how downcast she appeared, but he didn't say anything. Emma found she didn't have much appetite. She took small helpings of everything, only what she knew she could manage. Mrs. Wallace didn't like wasted food.

Back in their room, Juan quizzed her about what had happened during the day to make her so miserable. Sad-eyed, she looked at her companion. "You're going to hate me."

"No I won't. What has happened?"

Her voice barely above a whisper, Emma recounted her tale of falling asleep and letting the tub overflow into the kitchen below and being revealed as a girl to their landlady.

"Is that all?" chuckled Juan.

"You won't think it's so funny when I tell you that we have to move by the end of the week," Emma sniveled as she bent her head and held it in her hands. Her tears fell like a waterfall.

Juan slide to her side, wrapping his arms around her. "Now, now, it's not as bad as all that. We'll be all right." Taking his red handkerchief from his back pocket, he handed it to her. "Here, use my dirty hankie to dry your tears."

A weak laugh erupted as Emma elbowed him. "Who taught you that saying?"

Chuckling, Juan pulled Emma closer, squeezing her as he did. "I adore you, don't you know? I've learned a lot from observing your papa."

Chapter 9

• • • • • • •

Colorado to Idaho

Emma was finishing an order for a customer when Juan entered the store. She smiled as he approached the counter. "May I help you, sir?"

Glancing around, Juan drew closer and, lowering his voice. "Can you get away for a moment outside?"

"Oh, you have a question about the display in front? Let's step outside."

The two left the store, pretending to look at the fresh vegetables. Bubbling over with excitement, Juan said, "I have a job for us both that will take us all the way to Idaho. Pays our way and all. Isn't that great! We have to leave on the early-morning train tomorrow. Do you think you can leave here on short notice?"

Emma kept her eyes on the vegetables and gestured with her hands as if answering questions. Eyes alight, she murmured, "Of course I can quit here if it means getting to Idaho." Glancing through the window, she spied the manager walking toward the front door. "Sorry we don't have the vegetables you want. Check later in the week. We have a shipment coming in tomorrow."

Under her breath, she added, "I'll quit after my shift today. See you at home."

When Emma arrived at the boarding house, Juan was already packing. He nodded to her as she closed the door, and she couldn't miss his elation. "This is such a great opportunity for us. It just fell into my lap, so to speak."

"What does the job entail?" Emma asked, heading toward her meager belongings.

"We'll be caring for thoroughbred horses from Springer's on their way to their new owner's horse ranch near Mountain Home, Idaho." Breathless, he continued, "The men hired to travel with them quit. I don't know why, but Springer asked me to go and stay with the new owner, Kitty Wilkins, until she's familiar with the Oldenburg horses. He's agreed to pay your way if you'll help me."

"Sounds good. How many horses? Are they gigantic creatures? Will I be frightened? I don't think I've ever seen a warmblood. Do we have a place to sleep? Will we get our meals?"

"Stop asking questions—give me a chance to answer," chortled Juan, facing her. Raising one hand to his forehead, he said, "The horses are about this high," motioned Juan, "And as muscular as our working mules on the ranch. They're beautiful creatures. You'll get along fine with them because they respond readily to sweet talk." He flicked his eyebrows at the last remark, ducking as a pillow suddenly flew in his direction. "You won't be throwing anything but hay at me on the train. We'll be sleeping with the horses in our sleeping rolls."

Emma stopped and stared at him. "You mean we'll be in an open car with the horses? No seats? No bathroom? No decent bed? Just hay?"

"Yep," Juan answered, grinning from ear-to-ear as he watched Emma plunk herself down on the side of the bed. "Just remember we're working off the fare to Idaho. It won't be as bad as you think. There will be stops along the way when we'll get out to fetch water for the horses. It's true we'll be mucking out the car, but I'll do that."

"I thought we had saved just about enough for our Idaho train fare. Why do this?"

Shrugging his shoulders, Juan muttered just loud enough so Emma could hear, "A penny saved is a penny earned."

Shaking her head, Emma stood up. "Guess you're right. We should save as much as we can. We don't know how long it's going to take to track Papa down in Idaho." Spreading out her bedroll on top of the innerspring mattress, she began placing her few belongings neatly on top of it. "Packing won't take long. I haven't much."

❧

Arriving at the train station feeding lot just as the sun rose over the tops of the nearby buildings, Emma looked to Juan for direction about stashing her bedroll. "Guess we start work now," she commented.

"Good morning." Springer greeted them with a slightly southern twang. Dressed in a stylish riding outfit, including highly polished boots up to his knees, he carried a fancy riding crop he flicked on his right calf as he crossed the lot toward them. "Thank you for being on time. If you'll guide the horses down to the waiting boxcar, we'll be loaded in no time. The train doesn't leave for an hour, but I want the horses settled in before that."

As Emma grabbed for the lead line of a horse, a hand gripped her outstretched arm. Startled, she jerked as she turned toward the hand's owner. "What—? What are *you* doing here?" asked a shocked Emma.

A sober Wolfe looked down at her. Releasing her arm, he nodded for her to move away from the horses. "We need to talk."

"I can't. I have a job to do."

"This can't wait. It won't take but a moment of your precious time."

Leading two horses, Juan walked up to the pair. "Wolfe! What are you doing here?" Noticing Wolfe's expression, he stopped. "What's happened?"

"Look, Fritz sent me." Hesitating, he glanced down at the sawdust at his feet as he dug a hole with the toe of his boot. Looking up, he said, "Emma, your papa's in a hospital. He's in bad shape. I've been sent to escort you to him."

Juan dropped the leads he held and reached for Emma as she slumped. Wolfe grabbed her arm. With each of them steadying her, she allowed the two to prop her up. "I'll be okay. Just give me a moment."

"Sure. Just let us get you out of the way of the horses," muttered Juan. He and Wolfe, one on each side, helped her over to the gate of the fenced area. "You'll be all right here? I better get back to loading the horses. You stay with her." Juan nodded to Wolfe as he moved back toward the waiting horses. Grabbing the closest lead, he moved toward the open boxcar. As he did so, he couldn't help glimpsing back over his shoulder at Emma. How was this news going to affect Emma, especially if her papa was seriously injured?

As Juan left the boxcar to get more horses, he noticed

that Wolfe and Emma seemed to be arguing. She was gesturing frantically with her hands and shaking her head. Wolfe just stood there, looking down and repeatedly digging the toe of his boot into the ground, a habit of Wolfe's when dealing with a stubborn Emma. *She must be giving him a hard time*, thought Juan as he led the horses toward the train.

Chapter 10

• • • • • • • •

Heartbreak Trip

Suddenly their plans changed. Wolfe joined Emma and Juan in caring for the horses after Mr. Springer gave permission for the free helper. The six stalls in the boxcar took up only half the space, leaving plenty of room for hay, oats, and straw where the three could lounge and sleep.

Fear gripped Emma as she rubbed down one of the Oldenburgs before beginning to brush him. "Please let me reach Papa in time," she prayed aloud as she massaged the horse. His ears pricked up, and the horse turned his head toward her, giving her a nuzzle.

After the train left Denver and the stock car's motion steadied, Wolfe repeated the wording in the telegram concerning Papa. The information was concise; telegrams tended to be brief since the charge was for the number of words sent. Evidently, Papa tried to stop a runaway team in a town called Emmett. He'd been trampled by the horses, as well as run over by the wagon wheels. He was alive but in a coma.

As the train rumbled along, occasionally tooting its

horn to scare off a lone animal on the track, Emma nestled in a hollow of straw she'd created, not unlike those farm animals make for themselves, praying and thinking. On either side of her lounged Juan and Wolfe, both chewing pieces of straw. Deep in thought, she didn't pay attention to their conversation until Wolfe nudged her foot. "Are you taking a siesta?"

Glancing at both friends, Emma shook her head. "No, I'm not sleeping, just thinking."

"Well, you've missed our discussion about what to do when we reach Mountain Home," replied Wolfe.

"What about Mountain Home?" asked Emma.

"That's where our journey ends," replied Juan, removing the straw from his mouth. "The horses are to be delivered there and then taken to the Wilkins Ranch in Owyhee County in the southwest of Idaho."

"You have to get to Emmett pronto from there," added Wolfe. "But first we have to help Juan with the horses."

"I can't wait. I've got to get to Papa as soon as possible," Emma stated frantically. "It shouldn't take three to drive six horses to a ranch."

"Be reasonable, Emma. I signed on for both of us to deliver these horses to the Wilkins Ranch. It earned both of us our free ride to Idaho. I can't duck out on a promise. Either you go or Wolfe, that's the deal. You wouldn't want me to break my word?" countered Juan.

Emma nodded. "But my conscience tells me to get to Papa as soon as possible, even if I have to travel alone."

"It will all work out, I promise," said Juan, taking her hand in his. "Just have faith. Besides, Wolfe will join you as soon as he is able."

Emma watched Wolfe turn toward Juan with a

suspicious look. *Do these two know something they haven't told me?* Pondering whether to ask them directly, she considered the fact that Juan, who frequently predicted future events, might think Papa was already dead. Or was she reading more into the situation than she should?

With a squeal, the train slid to a stop. What the—? Emma wondered, trying to see through the slats what had caused the train to stop suddenly. Juan opened the stock car door to find cattle pressed close to their car. He could have stepped right onto their backs if they hadn't been milling in a frenzy. Several men on horseback appeared, trying to jockey the cattle away from the train. Hundreds of cattle were crunched together, with too few horsemen trying to control them. Emma watched in dismay as the cattle outmaneuvered the riders. As soon as they moved a group of cattle away from the train, others took their place. Soon a few train employees joined the effort to drive the cattle off by waving their hats, but even that failed.

Emma suddenly became aware of Juan and Wolfe nudging each other. Then each turned, grabbed saddles and rope, mounted an Oldenburg, and with a "Yippee," they vaulted out into an opening that appeared. Ropes in hand, the experienced New Mexican pair made short work of the situation with the help of the other cowboys, rounding up the beasties and moving them away from the train.

Laughing uproariously after their return, Juan and Wolfe pounded each other on the back. They helped Emma wipe down the two warmbloods and gave each a helping of grain. Smiling like two mischievous boys, they recalled the looks on the cowboys' faces when they'd emerged from the stock car.

"I think they thought we were spirits from heaven."

"Or maybe from another world," joked Juan, slapping Wolfe on the back.

Laughing, both wrestled each other onto the straw. "Join us, Emma," invited Wolfe, patting a spot next to him.

"Not in a wrestling match—no way." Emma giggled, turning her back on them.

❊

Soon the train pulled into a pint-size station. As soon as the doors slid open, a bucket brigade was organized to haul water for the horses. After the first couple of buckets, Emma learned how to hand them off without getting drenched. Before the conductor yelled, "All aboard," Wolfe scurried off and purchased sandwiches and enough apples for everyone, including the six horses.

After the hurried water brigade, Emma eagerly sought her nest in the straw, happy for a rest and a bite to eat. Juan and Wolfe leaned on one of the stalls, munching their sandwiches and chatting between bites.

"This Wilkins Horse Company where you're delivering these horses must be the famous horse dealer I've heard so much about," Wolfe commented.

"Yes, it's one of the best-known equine enterprises in our country, as well as internationally. The ranchland, according to what I heard, supports over ten thousand horses. They ship thousands of horses all over the country. The army is one of its biggest customers."

"Boy, Juan, what an opportunity for you. You're interested in animal breeding."

"Yaw, I can't believe my luck. I hope to meet Kittie

Wilkins, the daughter of the owner, who oversees most the breeding. She's developed topnotch stock from Clydesdales, Percherons, and Morgans. Now she's going to try her luck with these Oldenburgs."

Wolfe looked over at Juan, wondering if he was considering remaining at the Wilkins Ranch. It certainly would give him great experience in the field of animal breeding, his chief interest. *Mmm*, thought Wolfe. Might that give him the opening with Emma that he needed? Before now, he hadn't thought he had any chance with her, but maybe he did.

❁

As the engine approached Mountain Home and began to slow down, with a heavy heart Emma rolled up her bedroll. Juan and Wolfe scurried around, preparing to unloading the horses. With a jerk and a screech, the stock car slid to a halt. Before they could reach the door it opened, revealing a blue-eyed blond woman, impeccably dressed in a navy blue tailored riding attire and a matching broad-brimmed felt hat, astride a golden palomino.

The three unwashed, grubby, and bedraggled occupants of the stock car stared at the female in front of them. None had any prior experience of how to react, so they just stared. Emma was pleased she didn't burst out in giggles to cover her embarrassment, her usual reaction to unfamiliar situations.

"Welcome to Mountain Home. I hope you enjoyed the trip from Denver with my Oldenburg horses. I'm Kittie Wilkins of Wilkins Ranch. I couldn't wait to see my beauties, so I rode ahead."

Juan cleared his throat as he leaned over and held out his hand. "Glad to meet you, madam. I'm Juan." Nodding to his friends, he added, "This here is Emma, and that's Wolfe. He came along because he delivered news to Emma back in Denver that her papa was in a coma in Emmett. As you can imagine, she's in a hurry to reach her papa."

Facing Emma, Kittie said with authority, "We best get you back on this train before it leaves. Wolfe, go purchase tickets for the both of you. Tell the conductor that Kitty Wilkins requests that he hold the train until you two are on board." Nodding toward the station, she added, "Emma, you may wish to use the washroom before you get back on the train. Juan and I will take care of my horses."

"But don't you need Wolfe to help move the Oldenburgs to the ranch?" asked Emma.

"No, no. Don't you worry about a thing. Juan and I can manage," Kittie said. She dismounted and threw the reins over her horse's neck.

Leaving the washroom, Emma felt more refreshed. She walked toward Wolfe, who had cleaned some of the grime from his face. "I got us tickets, and they're waiting on us to board so we better hurry. That Kittie Wilkins must be some horse queen around here to be able to dictate the train schedule."

Chapter 11

• • • • • • • •

1911 Boise, Idaho

Jamie stood in the downstairs hall outside the music room listening to the notes of Schubert's "Valse Sentimentale." After moving into the house, one of the joys of home ownership he'd discovered was hearing Liz practicing daily, sometimes even after he'd slipped off to bed, tired from a long workday. Still troubled that her past remained a blank, she appeared to find great solace in music. Hearing the piece end, he stepped into the room before she could begin another. "That was lovely. Is it one you're going to play for our guests this afternoon?"

Liz left the grand piano and walked across the room toward him. "Yes. I thought I might play all Schubert compositions today." Brushing past him, she headed for the door. "I think I'd better check on dinner. Our guests will be arriving soon."

Jamie nodded and followed her out of the room, part of the way down the central hall. "I'll be in my office," he remarked. "I have business that needs attention."

"Need any help?" inquired Liz as she entered

the oversized kitchen at the rear of the house. The kitchen, remodeled by Jamie himself, looked more like a fancy restaurant kitchen than one usually found in a farmhouse. When they entertained, which they did frequently, especially on Sundays, Dora the cook hired several of her relatives to come in and help prepare the meal and serve. Glancing around, Liz observed that Dora's sisters were intent on various preparations for the forthcoming meal.

Dora glanced up at Liz's question, one she usually asked, never expecting an answer. When she was hired by Jamie Wester, he'd explained that his sister Liz didn't know the first thing about cooking unless given directions. The fact that she didn't cook nor did any housework didn't bother Dora. It was quite obvious that Liz had always lived a "kept" life.

Dora, who had just turned twenty-five, grew up on a nearby farm along with five brothers and six sisters. As the eldest, she'd learned early to care for her siblings. That included cooking for the family. Her mother worked alongside her father on their 160-acre homestead near Montour. When Jamie had advertised for a cook, Dora applied and was hired immediately. By then she knew life offered more than winters in a small, crowded four-room house and summers in a tent surrounded by sheep. She wanted a home and family of her own.

Sundays at the Westers' were special, even for the hired cook. Everyone's favorite meal, the same every week: fried chicken, mashed potatoes, chicken gravy, string beans, coleslaw, freshly baked rolls, and apple pie, came together like clockwork. All the vegetables came directly from their own garden, which Jamie tenderly nurtured in his off hours. He also cultivated an orchard close to the garden so the bees could service both. He'd purchased several hives from local farmers. He was anxious for the farm to be self-sufficient.

Jamie insisted large pitchers of milk be on the table. No beer. He said, "I smell enough of that at work." Most of his guests agreed milk was best. A diverse group of people from all walks of life found themselves at his Sunday table: politicians, shop owners, clergy, farmers, miners, waitresses, paperboys, and bankers plus their wives and children were invited to dine. It made for a large group, but both Jamie and Liz enjoyed lively discussions at the dining table. Sometimes it became rather raucous, especially when the talk turned to politics. When the discussion became too loud, Liz always found a way to move the adults into the parlor for music and the children outside for games.

Liz seemed to enjoyed the Sundays when Dillon attended their gatherings. She loved listening to him tell Jamie about the many interesting events of rural Idaho life. His own eighty acres included an Indian trail crossing from one corner to another. Even in 1911 a few Indians still used the trail as they traveled from their summer hunting grounds to their winter home. Dillon allowed them to camp near the two-story barn he'd erected. By happenstance he'd built the barn across their old path. The Indians were friendly and loved to sit around in the evening and tell stories about the good old days.

Dillon was proud of his barn, which he'd designed with Jamie's help. It served as a shelter for his animals on the ground level, as well as his home on the upper level. He had two rooms; one served as his kitchen/sitting area, and the other was for sleeping. The heat from the animals below warmed the living area above. According to Jamie, this was a common practice in the old countries, especially Germany. The building was snug and warm during the winter, and when opened up in the summer the breezes blew through, making the space cool and comfortable.

Out past the barn to the west stood the old well, operated by a tall windmill. This had been on the property when he bought it. He'd kept the windmill despite Jamie's insistence that it needed a lot of repairs. Beyond the well, at some distance, Dillon built a two-seater outhouse, painted red to match the barn, with a quarter-moon cutout in the door. Farther from the outhouse, he'd built his chicken coop.

On Jamie's advice, Dillon left space between the barn and the road leading to Boise and Emmett. Plans for a four-room house he'd build once he married and started a family were in the works, whenever that would be. So far, starting the apple orchard had kept him too busy to concentrate on finding a mate, though he looked at the small local church he attended every Sunday.

Jamie and he had been part of the gang of locals that constructed the building now used not only as a church but also as a school. Every Sunday various ministers from different faiths visited their small church to provide religious instruction for the families who attended. They were served alternatively by Methodists, Baptists, Holy Rollers, and Mormons. Dillon enjoyed the lively Sundays when the Holy Roller minister came. Music was provided by a young housewife, Harriet, one of the farmer's wives, who also headed of the Sunday school program. She was very good on the pump organ.

But all the young women attending the church were

married; Dillon was the lone bachelor. Only when he visited Jamie and Liz in Boise did he meet unattached women. As frequently as he could, he traveled to Boise, but it wasn't often enough to make a real connection with any particular young lady.

Chapter 12

• • • • • • •

On to Emmett

Emma and Wolfe quickly found seats together midway down the car. Emma claimed the window seat. The scruffy-looking interior of the car needed a good cleaning, she observed, but theorized that she fit right in since she still wore her dirt-caked clothing that reeked of horse.

"Wow, they really are in a hurry to leave," remarked Wolfe as the train's motion thrust him into his seat. He almost missed the rack above as he flung their bedrolls up.

Emma nodded and turned toward the window. "Thank goodness Kittie Wilkins had them wait for us. We would have waited several hours for the next one."

Stretching out his legs and crossing them at his ankles, Wolfe tilted his hat down, as if intending to sleep. "Make yourself comfortable. We have a couple of hours before Emmett."

Heeding his suggestion, Emma removed her Stetson and combed her fingers through her mop; she shook her head to free the remaining plastered-down hairs. Feeling the sweat running down her backbone, she rubbed her back against her seat like dogs do to scratch themselves. Turning to Wolfe, who sat unmoving, she said, "Isn't this heat bothering you?"

Pushing his hat back with one finger, Wolfe grinned. "Heat? You going to let a little temperature bother you as you ride along in comfort?"

Elbowing him, Emma grimaced and used her hat as a fan. "Wish I had the fancy fan Caruso gave me."

"You mean the one you brought back from Corsicana after visiting him there? The time you almost fell to the main floor of the opera house from the balcony because your ankle twisted in your new high-heeled shoes?" Wolfe sat up straight and turned toward her. "I remember you telling me about your uncle holding onto your ankle until a tall musician caught you. What a miracle!"

Emma beamed at Wolfe. "I didn't think you'd remember that, or anything else I told you when we were children."

"I remember everything you told me. And, for that matter, everything we did back in Texas. You were the highlight of my childhood. Until we became friends, my life was boring. I did my farm chores, hunted and sold armadillos, fished, and went to school."

"Yes, and as I remember it, you played hooky from school a lot to go fishing."

Smiling warmly, Wolfe nodded. "School was dull, so lots of us kids played hooky. It was the thing to do."

"Do you remember your cave above the river?" asked Emma.

"Of course, do you recall us sharing it?"

Smiling, Emma fell silent as she visualized Wolfe's cave and the hours she'd spent nestled on the soiled and mildewed pillows, reading books and writing letters to Caruso. Thoughts of the cave brought back memories of the man Billy, who lived in the two-story cave. Billy saved them when they got stuck on the barn roof, where they'd sought safety from the mother boar.

"Wolfe, whatever happened to Billy, the man who lived in that two-story cave?"

Lightheartedness spread over Wolfe's demeanor as he stroked his chin. "The last I heard, Billy struck gold, so to speak, with his guided rafting tours and his boat rental business."

"Does he still live in his cave?"

"No, I think he lives someplace on the outskirts of New Braunfels."

Emma smiled. Then, suddenly, her face crumpled, and tears filled her eyes. Immediately Wolfe's arms enfolded her, pulling her against his chest. "There now, let it all out." Sobs wracked her entire body. She felt Wolfe pull her tightly against his body and feather-like kisses on the top of her head. "We'll get there in time. Don't worry."

Melting into his body, Emma gave into the tenderness he offered. It felt so good to be able to go with her feelings rather than considering what she should or shouldn't do. Wolfe's fingers gently rubbed and kneaded her back easing her stress. The tears subsided and the hiccups began. She started to rub the moisture from around her eyes, but Wolfe handed her his handkerchief, saying mischievously with a twinkle in his eye, "Here, use my snotty handkerchief."

Through teary eyes and unwelcome hiccups, Emma managed a feeble laugh at Wolfe's using her papa's traditional remark to lighten her spirit. Disentangling herself from him, she straightened up and peeked around to see if the other passengers had noticed her breakdown. Mama never allowed them to make a spectacle of themselves in public as she had just done. Like her papa would have, Wolfe patted her on the shoulder. "Never worry about what others think. Be true to yourself."

As they rode along in silence, Wolfe eventually slipped his hand into hers and gave two squeezes, signaling he cared. The two sat lost in their own thoughts. Quiet conversations could be heard throughout the car, along with an occasional childish outburst. Across the aisle, a woman knitted as she gazed out the window at the passing sagebrush. Ahead of them, a man rose and, holding the hand of his son, walked toward the front of the car.

"Emmett! Emmett coming up," the conductor called out as he walked through the car and into the next one.

Emma roused herself from her thoughts and squeezed the hand holding hers. "I'm so glad you came with me. I haven't traveled alone before, and it's a little scary not knowing what to expect."

Returning the squeeze with a slight shake, Wolfe rose and retrieved their belongings from the rack above. He hoisted everything onto his broad shoulders. Stepping back so Emma could follow him down the aisle, he maneuvered his way, careful not to hit others exiting the train.

As Emma walked off the train, she felt like she'd stepped into a hot oven. Staggering, she felt Wolfe's hand guide her forward, protecting her from the push of people behind. The small station building and the waiting people, wagons, mules, and horses clustered about hid the town from sight. They couldn't see anything. Taking the lead, Wolfe elbowed through the crowd toward the end of the station.

"I've been told the hospital is above the barbershop, beside Tollman's Hotel. Do you think you can walk into town?" asked Wolfe as he repositioned the bedrolls onto one shoulder so he could hold her hand as they walked.

Nodding, Emma walked beside him as they left the station, dodging the carriages and wagons leaving at a leisurely pace carrying noisy, excited passengers.

Chapter 13

• • • • • • • •

Finding Papa

Emma walked into a dimly lit wallpapered room so large that it overpowered the single brownish metal bed across from the door. The white-covered form on the bed lay motionless, looking more like bunched-up pillows with a sheet thrown over them than a body. Startled by the silence and overwhelming antiseptic odor, Emma conscientiously fought for control of herself. Holding back her mounting anguish, she slowly stepped toward the head of the bed, murmuring, "Papa, it's me. It's Emma." His eye lids were closed but visible through slits in the surrounding bandages. There was no response to her greeting.

"You must be the daughter," came a voice from behind her. Emma turned toward a solemn-looking, tallish man in a three-piece tweed suit. "I'm Doctor Clarke. So glad you're here. We've been hoping and praying a family member would come."

After greeting the doctor, Emma stepped aside to allow him to move close to the bedside. She watched as he placed his stethoscope on Papa's taped chest after pulling the sheet away. She watched him listen first to his heart and then his lungs. The doctor sighed to himself as he moved to the bandaged head, lifting first one eyelid and then the other. Finally, he turned away from his patient and faced her. "Let's go out into the hall so I can fill you in on how your father is doing."

Before following the doctor, she turned to Papa. "I'll be right back, Papa." Patting where his shoulder must be, she turned, almost falling over a straight-back chair she hadn't noticed. Inhaling, she righted herself and headed for the door outlined by the hall light beyond.

A short distance outside the door the doctor stopped and waited for her. "As you can see, your father's in a coma, but his heart's strong. His breathing is labored because he can only take in half the oxygen his body needs. Several of his limbs and his ribs were crushed by the wagon wheels. Thankfully his backbone didn't suffer any permanent damage, so he should be able to walk. His skull's bruised and his brain swollen. That's why he's in a coma. It's nature's way of healing."

"Can he hear me while he's in a coma?"

"Yes, he can hear us all, but he especially will be tuned into your voice. You need to talk to him so he's encouraged to awaken. You can give him a reason to fight for consciousness."

Emma listened intently to what the doctor said. Shifting her eyes downward, she asked, "Does he have a chance?"

"Yes, he does, but it's up to him and the Lord. You must do all you can to give him the incentive to awaken. I've treated many who have been in comas for years and then suddenly awakened. There's always hope."

Did she have the persistence to do all that the doctor

suggested? Yes, of course she did. She'd never given up believing that Papa had survived the San Francisco earthquake and would return for her. He'd come back to her. But now God once again seemed to be testing her faith. Jerked back to the present, she nodded to the doctor. "I'll do my best." Inwardly, she questioned her resolve.

"I'll check in every day during my rounds. If you need me, my office is upstairs in the bank building on Main and Washington."

Standing alone with her thoughts after the doctor walked away, Emma's attention was attracted by a boisterous couple entering the second floor of the building after climbing the stairs. The man wore denim pants held up by colorful suspenders, a faded blue buttoned long-sleeve cotton shirt underneath. The woman clutched a long garment over one arm. Her wind-blown hair hung wildly over the collar of a plain black shirtwaist. A gathered reddish plaid skirt showing her ankles completed her outfit. The two stopped the doctor walking toward them, asking, "Are you the doctor? We're here about Dillon. How's he doing?"

As Emma turned back toward the room where Papa lay, she caught a side view of the woman talking to the doctor. A quiver shot through her body. Walking toward her papa's bed, she thought to herself that she must be hungry to shiver like that. When was the last time she'd eaten? The chill didn't last long, so she dismissed it, reminding herself that she and Wolfe should try to eat just as soon as he returned from getting rooms at the hotel.

Pulling the straight-backed chair over to the bed, Emma sat down facing her papa. The doctor had said he'd been unconscious since they'd brought him into the hospital. How long was that? Counting back from the time Wolfe had received the telegram and then found her, plus their travel time, it must be several weeks. "Oh, Papa, please wake up. I need you. Don't leave me."

Reaching under the sheet, Emma grasped her papa's hand and lifted it toward her. Leaning over, she kissed the familiar long, graceful fingers. "Oh, Papa, you just have to wake up. You're all I've got now. You're my only family." Burying her face in his open hand, she began to pray.

"Lord, please heal Papa. I need him. He's all I've got. The doctor says he has several broken bones and a concussion. As the Master Physician of all mankind who can heal, please, if it is your wish to do so, heal my papa. Yes, I know you can say no, but I'm asking you to heal Papa so I can take him home to New Mexico. I promise to take good care of him and be a good daughter. Please, in the name of Jesus Christ Our Lord. Amen."

"How's he doing?" asked Wolfe as he entered the room after she'd finished her prayer. She looked up at him, and the expression on her face answered his question. Placing his hand on her shoulder, he gave a squeeze as he looked at the unresponsive figure on the bed. It was difficult to comprehend that the gentle man he knew as Bruno was the same as the person on the bed. He considered asking her what the doctor had said but decided against it. Emma was in no condition to repeat the probably disappointing news to him, at least not now. He had to support her and keep her spirits up. That was his job.

Chapter 14

• • • • • • •

Strangers

Soon after receiving the news from an Emmett client that Dillon had been injured while working on his well and taken to the local hospital, Jamie picked Liz up from their house. They headed out of Boise in his black two-seater Ford. Concerned for his friend, Jamie couldn't help but notice Liz's reaction to the news they'd received. Between tears and hiccupping, she created a pile of wet handkerchiefs on the floor of his vehicle. Although they traveled at top speed, the thirty miles seemed more like a hundred. Liz kept asking, "He'll be okay, won't he?"

As he drove along the monotonous road, he let his mind wonder. Thinking back over the years that had passed since leaving San Francisco with Liz, he realized how accustomed he'd become to having her around, like her being beside him now. He enjoyed their daily conversations that kept him challenged intellectually, although he'd never admit it. She brought laughter into his life, and she was someone other than himself to care about. She was his mainstay, but he couldn't admit that to her. He was afraid of revealing his true feelings to anyone, especially Liz, for fear of getting hurt again. After his experience with Peg, he'd promised himself he would never open his heart again to anyone. The pain of rejection was so intense that it was difficult to transfer the allegiance he'd once conferred on a person he thought loved him. No, he could never allow that.

"We're almost there. Should we go directly to the hospital or stop and get a reservation at the hotel?" Liz's question jarred Jamie back to the present.

Glancing at her, he replied, "I recall Dillon mentioning that the local doctors use the rooms over the barbershop in the center of town as a hospital. We can get hotel reservations later."

"Shouldn't we stop and ask for directions?"

"Mmm, I think I can find it without asking. It's a small town."

Jamie saw Liz shrug her shoulders, probably in exasperation. Why was it that she always wanted to ask for directions from others rather than depending on him? He had a good sense of direction, always had since boyhood. Hadn't his family relied on him to locate places they were seeking for the first time? Why hadn't Liz learned this about him after the five years they'd been together?

A smile crept across Jamie's face as he recalled his parents arguing over silly little things like where to stop for a picnic lunch or where to park in town while they shopped. His mom never agreed with his dad but always gave in to him, saying, "Let's not fuss but enjoy whatever we do."

"We're here," Jamie announced, turning off the engine. Reaching out, he cupped Liz's hand in his and gave it a squeeze. "He's going to be fine, I just know it.

Don't worry." Stepping out of the car, he walked around and opened the door for her.

He'd stopped before a two-story building with a rotating candy-striped cylinder advertising a barbershop. Jamie knew he was in the right place. He spotted an outside stairway that must lead to where the town's doctors had their hospital for critically ill or injured patients.

"I think we go through the door up there," said Jamie, motioning toward a door at the top of a flight of wooden stairs. After climbing only a few steps, the smell of disinfectant assailed them. Sniffing, Jamie said, "Yes, this is the place."

After stepping into the building, Jamie intercepted a man with a stethoscope around his neck walking toward them. As Jamie talked to the doctor, he noticed Liz's gaze following a young woman who disappeared into a room. Liz almost immediately began rubbing both arms as if she were cold. *How strange*, he thought before he turned his concentration back to what the doctor was telling him.

"So, other than a broken leg and fractured wrist, he's okay?" asked Jamie.

Nodding, the doctor turned toward Liz to include her. "Yes, there's no indication of any internal injuries. However, I'd like to keep him here a day or two to make certain. We've got empty beds, only one is occupied by a critically ill patient," he stated. "Your friend will need care after being discharged because that leg will be in a cast for a least a month."

Giving Liz a knowing glance, Jamie said, "That won't be any problem. We'll probably take him back to Boise with us."

Dr. Clarke nodded. "I'll see you tomorrow. He should be able to leave in the next few days if no complications crop up."

Placing his hand under Liz's elbow, Jamie guided her down the hall toward Dillon's room. "Here we are, you old steeple climber. Can't resist climbing anything taller than you, can you? How many times is it now with a broken leg?"

A chuckle came from the person on the bed. "Well, look who pried themselves out of the bowels of Boise. Couldn't resist coming and teasing me about my fall from grace."

Liz elbowed Jamie before walking to the bedside. "Tell me how on earth you did this to yourself and why."

"Pull up a chair." Dillon nodded toward a decrepit-looking upholstered armchair against the wall. As Liz pulled the chair close to the bed, Dillan worked himself up till he was sitting. Adjusting a pillow under the leg in the cast, he smiled at his friends. *How nice to have visitors,* he thought. Since arriving at the hospital, he'd only seen the doctor and one nurse. He wasn't used to being immobile. He was grateful the nurse had provided him with a long-necked bottle so he could pee on his own. Rousing from his thoughts, he looked first at Liz and then at Jamie. He felt himself relax.

"So, you're curious about my fall," he stated in a teasing voice. "Well, let me tell you of a farmer who discovered one morning that he couldn't pump water for his animals or himself. He had a problem. Was his well dry, or was something wrong with his pump? First, he opened the well and put down a bucket. There was water. So it was the windmill. Up he climbed, checking at each level that the old wood structure wasn't rotten. But lo and behold, at the very top he discovered dry rot, or you might say it found him. *Wham!* he found himself falling to the ground. One leg broken and a wrist smashed. End of story." With twinkling eyes, grinning broadly like an eight-year old kid, Dillan looked at his audience.

"You always were a storyteller," remarked Jamie as he removed his hands from his pockets. Feigning a scowl, he shoved a second straight-back chair up to the bed and straddled it. "I thought you checked the windmill before you bought the place. Didn't I tell you to?"

"I did. I climbed up once. Seemed okay then. Guess I should have put it on my yearly 'to-do list'."

"I'm just glad you're not badly hurt," commented Liz. "You could have killed yourself." She leaned forward and gave Dillon's arm a squeeze. "We'll check in at the Tollman Hotel next door for the night. Just as soon as you're discharged, we'll take you home with us. Won't we?" she asked, looking over at Jamie.

"Of course, we'll look after you while you recuperate."

"I can manage at my place. Besides, there's the animals to consider. I'll do just fine with a crutch."

"No, you won't," interjected Liz. "Your living area is upstairs in the barn. How do you expect to manage the ladder?" Drawing a breath, she looked over at Jamie for support. "I can stay with you if you insist on going back to your place."

Shaking his head, Dillan declared, "No!" He angrily threw up his hands. "Around here, neighbors help neighbors. At this very moment, George and his son Lawson are repairing the water pump. The son has offered to take care of my livestock and gardens until I'm back on my feet. George's daughter Lilly is going to come in daily and fix meals for me. Everything's been taken care of. I don't need your help, thank you."

Jamie and Liz exchanged glances. Dillon was being very independent about all this. It was obvious that he didn't want any help from them. Gesturing with his hands, Jamie surrendered. "Have it your way. Can we at least stay until you're discharged?"

Sinking back and pulling the sheet up, Dillon nodded. He agreed to that but not to having Liz stay with him. He couldn't have her that near day and night without breaking his oath to himself not to reveal to her his true feelings. When she'd helped him in the kitchen in Seattle, he'd developed a fondness for her. It hadn't taken long for that fondness to turn into strong feelings of protectiveness. He found himself in love. Upon their arrival in Boise, he realized that he had to put some distance between them. She obviously favored Jamie over him, even though Jamie continuously put developing his business ahead of any commitment to her. Sneaking a look at Liz, he was startled to see disappointment on her face. Could she have feelings for him, he wondered.

Walking to the end of the bed, Jamie said, "Liz, I think we'd better take our leave and let Dillon rest. We'll be back in the morning. Sleep well, my friend. Want us to bring you anything?"

"A new leg and wrist would be nice."

Chapter 15

• • • • • • • •

Letter from Juan

Dear Emma,

This Kittie I'm working for is some lady. She's the undisputed boss of the Diamond Ranch and aptly named the Horse Queen of Idaho, with her own registered brand that is recognized as signifying reliable horse stock. She got her start by rounding up wild horses on the range between Nevada's Humboldt River and Idaho's Snake River. By law, the mustangs became the property of anyone who could catch and brand them. She captured all the unbranded mustangs she could, thousands, and she was in business. Anyway, I've just finished six hours on the backs of several mustangs, breaking them. My poor body is rebelling at the beating it has taken, but I know as I continue doing this, my body will toughen-up. How I wish I could enjoy a meal with you rather than ten cowboys who talk of nothing but going to town and getting drunk. A conversation with you would lighten my heart and soul. I pray that your papa's healing and soon will be out of the hospital.

Hugs to my New Mexico gal,
Juan,

Chapter 16

• • • • • • •

Bedside

One day while reading to her father *The Secret Garden* by Frances Burnett, a recently published novel that she'd been itching to read because the story was much like her own, a woman she had never seen before stepped into the room.

"Do you mind having a visitor?"

Looking up from her book, Emma smiled. "Of course not. Please come in. We'd welcome a visitor." Emma stood to face the mysterious woman. "Please have a seat."

"I just wanted to come and see how your father's doing. You know, he visited me the day before his accident."

"No, I didn't know that," commented Emma, pushing back a stray hair from her forehead. "Would you mind telling me what the visit was about?"

Chuckling, the woman smiled demurely. "Well ..." She attempted to find a comfortable way to answer the question. "Let me introduce myself. I'm Mrs. Cummings, wife of Dr. Cummings. Around here I'm known as the local concert pianist."

"Oh!" exclaimed Emma. "If you're a musician, I'll bet my papa thought you might be my mama, his wife, who disappeared after the San Francisco earthquake."

"Yes, you're correct. I guess he'd heard about me and thought I might be her. We had a lengthy conversation over cups of tea about the family, your parents growing up in Texas, he on a farm and she at an orphanage in town. He told me about their trip to San Francisco to celebrate their anniversary." She stopped before mentioning that he'd talked about her lost brother. She placed her hand on Emma's shoulder. "You know, don't you, he is proud of you and your mastery of the violin just to please him?"

"How sad for Papa. He really thought he'd found Mama at last."

"I know. He left my house very despondent. Said he'd be traveling back to Santa Fe in a couple of days. Such a tragedy that the very next day he was trampled by a team of runaway horses and buggy. Thank goodness it happened not far from Dr. Clarke's office and he was in attendance or it might have been worse for your father."

"Yes, I hear that may have saved his life," commented Emma, turning to look at her papa.

She shifted uneasily in her chair as she observed the compassionate expression on her visitor's face. As the silence lengthened, Mrs. Cummings rose. "Emma, if there is anything I can do for you, please do not hesitate to call on me. Perhaps you would consider staying at our house until your father's out of his coma and can travel. We would love to have you."

Emma looked up at the elegantly dressed woman

standing beside the bed. Her thinking was muddled since she'd heard why her papa visited Emmett. What had the doctor's wife suggested? Oh yes, that she could stay at her house while Papa recovered. Now she slept on the floor beside his bed in her sleeping roll to save money. The barber had offered her one of the empty patient rooms close by, but she'd turned him down. She'd wired Fritz for money, but it hadn't arrived. Thank goodness Juan and Wolfe had loaned her a few dollars so she had money for food.

Startled from her thoughts, Emma murmured, "Thank you so much for the offer, but I'd rather stay close to Papa. Please come and visit again. You've been so nice." As an afterthought, she mustered a weak smile.

※

"Emma, many weeks have passed without improvement in your father's condition," said Doctor Clarke. "I think we must consider transferring him to a hospital in Boise. I have spoken with Doctor John Springer, who used to practice here in Emmett but has since moved to Boise. He agrees that your father may have a better chance there. I have reserved a private room for him at St. Luke's Episcopal Hospital."

Emma nodded and dabbed her eyes with a handkerchief. She had become discouraged as the days passed without signs of improvement. Papa was becoming a skeleton right under her nose. For that matter, Wolfe had scolded her just the other day for not eating enough. He didn't like to see her clothes hanging loosely from her shoulders.

Suddenly she became aware that Doctor Clarke was speaking to her.

"I've arranged for a horse-drawn ambulance from St. Luke's Hospital to transport him to Boise along with his nurse. You may ride along, too, if you like."

"Yes, of course I want to ride with him. When do we leave?"

"The ambulance should be here around noon. After the driver eats and the horses rest, you'll start for Boise." With that, Dr. Clarke turned from his patient. Facing Emma, he said, "When you get settled at St. Luke's, I suggest you think long and hard about an activity you and your father did together that might reach him and bring him out of his deep coma. Your reading and talking to him aren't doing all that they should. Since his wife played the piano, perhaps a musical piece, an instrument, a language other than English—anything to reach into the world he's trapped in—might jolt him into consciousness."

With little time to prepare for departure, Emma immediately sent a telegram to Uncle Fritz and messages to Juan and Wolfe so they'd know her whereabouts. Returning to Papa's room, she packed for both of them. For the first time in a long time she felt hopeful. Perhaps the change of care would improve his condition. In Boise, there would be more doctors to consult, as well as around-the-clock nursing staff. She wouldn't have to live in his room day and night.

As they made their way to Boise in the back of a semi-enclosed wagon drawn by two sturdy mules, Emma sat next to Papa's cot holding his hand. The ride went smoothly until they climbed a steep hill on the outskirts of town. Emma held her breath; would the straps hold the bed? She readied herself to grab Papa if he showed signs of slipping off the cot. Reaching the top, the driver stopped the team to let them rest. Emma gave a sigh of relief as she tidied the blanket around her papa. "That was quite a climb," she said. "Hope that's the only rough part of our trip."

After the ambulance team rested, the rest of the road into Boise was straight and flat. Emma found herself deep in thought about what the doctor had said to her. Thinking back over the last few years, she realized that other than her papa's involvement in the store and his pride in her violin playing ... Her violin! Suddenly she knew what to do. She'd get a violin and play for him. That would bring him out of his coma. Why hadn't she thought of that before? Pleased with herself, she began humming. Squeezing his hand, she leaned over close to his ear. "I know what to do. You'll be out of your coma as quick as I tune a violin."

The nurse who had traveled with the ambulance from Boise turned out to be a cheerful and attentive person. Emma was delighted. During their conversation, she learned there were several hotels, as well as boarding houses, close to the hospital where she might stay. The young nurse told her not to worry about getting around Boise. The city was quite progressive, with sidewalks, paved and named street, and streetcars. "We're as modern as San Francisco, Portland, and Seattle, the three largest cities on the West Coast," boasted the nurse.

❦

Before leaving for Boise, Emma received a postcard from Juan at the Diamond Ranch, but she hadn't had time to read it with all the preparations necessary for their departure. Pulling it out from her pocket now, she began to read.

Dearest Emma,

In the next few days I will be herding horses to Emmett for shipment to the cavalry stationed at Ft. Bliss. A Mexican by the name of Poncho Villa is stirring up trouble across the border, and they're getting prepared for a possible attack. Kittie has given me a few days off so I can see you. You are constantly in my thoughts and prayers.

See you soon,
Juan

Chapter 17

• • • • • • •

Boise

After spending all her time caring for papa in the one room in Emmett, Emma discovered the activity around Boise City raised her spirits, as well as renewed her enthusiasm for life. Being around people rather than sitting all the time with Papa, lightened her mood. Her appetite returned. She began to sing while walking, and she found she smiled more.

After much searching, she'd taken a small room at the Californian Hotel on Main Street for fifty cents a day, about the cheapest rate she'd found for a lady alone; however, expenses were mounting. Wolfe and Juan contributed their earnings to the money sent from Santa Fe, but it wasn't enough. She'd written to Uncle Fritz to send more but hadn't heard back from him. If more funds weren't forthcoming, she guessed she'd have to look for a job. Both Juan and Wolfe were against her doing so, arguing, "Your job is at your papa's bedside."

Stepping into her papa's room one morning, Emma sang out, "Morning, Papa! It's a beautiful day. There's not a cloud in the sky. I have a treat for you today, a new piece to play for you." She placed her violin case on the bottom of the bed and brought out the violin and bow. She'd been doing this for several days since she'd gotten the loan of the violin from a member of the Boise Symphony Orchestra. Tucking the violin under her chin, Emma tuned the strings, starting with E. Sighing, she glanced over at the bed. "I'll bet you'll remember this one. We heard it in San Francisco when Mama, Edmund, you, and I went to the opera to hear Caruso sing. It's the *Habanera*. After that announcement, she began to play softly so she didn't disturb other patients. In her mind's-eye she could see the stage at the opera house in San Francisco. She felt her Mama's presence and saw Papa's proud silhouette.

Finishing the music, she glanced at her father. No change. Not discouraged, she began playing some of her study pieces by Kayser from memory. She walked around the room, chin touching the violin slightly, right hand bowing. Her papa frequently urged her to practice the music he'd brought from New Braunfels to Santa Fe. He referred to them as his "musical musings," to be played when one wished to be lulled into a trance of beautiful notes and let one's fingers fly of their own accord over the strings. She could visualize him now in the music room at home, standing in the middle of the room, holding his violin, bow in hand, playing away with a dreamy expression on his face. She would give anything to see that look again.

Staring out the window, Emma continued playing. Suddenly she heard a sound behind her. Startled, she turned. "Sorry, I didn't mean to interrupt you. What were you playing? It was lovely," commented Juan. He threw his jacket over the chair before stepping to the bedside. "Any change?"

Tucking her violin under her right arm, she shook her head and shielding the violin, stepped into a one-armed hug. Her head sought the comfort of his shoulder. He planted a kiss on her cheek.

With another squeeze, Juan whispered, "He's going to come around. I just know it."

Stepping away, she asked, "But when? It's been so long."

"You can't give up hope now. You never did give up hope that he'd survived the earthquake, and you can't now. Where's my optimistic New Mexico gal?"

"She's still here," came the answer. She smiled as she poked him in the ribs. "I'm just tired, I guess."

"Well, let's go have a bite to eat. I'll bet you haven't eaten much today. Wolfe's talking to the doctor in the hall. After he's finished, we're taking you out to eat. You need a change of scenery and some fresh air." He raised his head slightly and wrinkled his nose as if he'd smelled something strange.

As the three friends exited the hospital into the sunlight, Emma shielded her eyes from the sun's rays. Recently leafed out trees cast dancing shadows on the newly mown grass and sidewalk around the hospital. As Emma took deep breaths of fresh air, she thought about how right Juan had been that she needed to get out into the open. Usually she rushed from the hotel to the hospital in the mornings, hardly noticing anything along the way. Her evening schedule was the same but in darkness.

Emma was so deep in thought as they walked, she would have missed the entrance to the café if Juan's hand on her elbow hadn't guided her. The trio settled into an empty table by the window. After ordering soup and bread, the daily luncheon special, the most economical of the offerings, Emma turned to Wolfe. "Did the doctor have anything new to report about Papa's condition?"

Swallowing, Wolfe shook his head. "No, I'm afraid he reports little change in your father's condition. But he cautioned again that with the type of injury he sustained, it may take months, even years, for your papa to come out of it."

Just then the waiter arrived, carrying their bowls of lentil soup and freshly baked bread slices. Both Juan and Wolfe began to dig into their food. Emma sat looking at the bowl in front of her. "What can we do? Nothing I do appears to reach him. I read and talk to him. I spend hours playing my violin for him, but it's not working."

Wolfe turned toward her. "You just have to be persistent and not give up hope." Continuing to eat, he gave Juan a knowing look. "I asked the doctor this morning if being in familiar surroundings like back home might help him. He thought it might. He will grant us permission to remove your father from the hospital if we take him home to New Mexico. Juan and I just have to figure out how to transport him that far in his present condition."

Emma looked from one to the other of her companions. She hadn't even considered taking Papa home. Absently, she took a bite of bread and then another. Being in his own home might be the solution. There'd be the smell of piñon everywhere, dry air and Aunt Maria's cactus jelly to put on his toast. On good days, he could sit or lie out on the patio in the sun. *Oh yes, that might just be what Papa needs to bring him out.* Putting her spoon down, she enthusiastically answered, "Yes, let's take Papa home. When can we leave?"

"Hold on. There are many problems to solve first."

Wolfe glanced at Juan, saying as he rubbed his chin, "I've spoken to Mr. French about leaving. He understands my position. We can leave just as soon as he's hired a replacement." Seeing how eager Emma was, Wolfe wondered if they'd been presumptuous about making the decision to go home without consulting Emma first?

Smiling, Juan added, "Kittie's willing to let me go if I can also find a replacement. We're in town now looking for unemployed cowboys." Wolfe nodded in agreement as he wiped his bowl clean with a piece of bread. "We're also investigating the best way to travel to Santa Fe. Did the doctor give you any ideas this morning when you talked to him, Wolfe?"

Placing his mug on the table, Wolfe replied, "Yes, he did. He didn't think the train would work because there aren't any Pullman cars available traveling in the direction we're going. He suggested a motorized truck, so Papa could lie down during the trip. We'd have to cover the truck bed to protect him from the elements. That would be no trouble." He looked at Juan. "But finding such a truck might pose a problem. I haven't seen many around but I could make some inquiries."

Looking from one to the other of her dearest friends, Emma said, "Going by a motorized contraption will be costly as well as time consuming. Couldn't we talk to train management and see if we can arrange for an entire train car for ourselves? With two adjoining seats, we could rig up a bed of sorts for Papa. Or what about a box car? Couldn't we set that up to work? You know, like we traveled from Denver in?" Asked Emma looking at Juan. "Papa's slept on many a straw bed, and so have we." She chuckled, looking from Juan to Wolfe. "It doesn't matter in Papa's condition. We can keep him comfortable. And we three can certainly rough it."

Chapter 18

• • • • • • •

Awake!

Emma had just finished playing the violin for Papa and was putting it away in its case when a woman she recognized as Mrs. Cummings of Emmett and another woman she didn't know entered the room. Smiling, she closed the case and faced her visitors.

"Good morning, Emma. Let me introduce a friend of mine, Liz Wester, who teaches piano here in Boise."

The woman approaching looked close to forty. She wore riding boots, a flowing black skirt, and a white shirtwaist with a black ribbon tie. Her hair covered one side of her face. She held her head slightly to the side. Pinned close to her left shoulder was a gold-etched watch on a chain, much like her mama and Tante Helga in Texas had worn. *Must be a sign of their musical profession,* Emma thought.

Upon first seeing the woman, Emma felt a shudder radiate from her neck down the center of her body, ending with a twinge in her knees. "How do you do," said Emma, noticing the semi-hidden scar on the woman's cheek that was revealed briefly as she'd moved toward her. "Do I know you? You look so familiar."

"I have the same feeling. I think we both spotted each other for just a moment at the Emmett Hospital many weeks ago. I was there to see an injured friend while your father was there."

"Oh, yes, I remember seeing you now," remarked Emma. "What brings you two here today?" asked Emma, looking from one to the other.

"First and foremost, I wanted to stop by and see how your father is doing. I promised Dr. Clarke I'd report back to him. Since Liz and I are giving a piano concert in the hospital chapel for the patients, I thought maybe we could get your father into a wheelchair so he could attend the performance. Maybe the music will wake him up."

Brightening, Emma nodded. "Sounds like a good idea. We've been getting him up and into a wheelchair a couple of days a week. He doesn't show it, but I think he enjoys being someplace other than flat on his back. Perhaps piano music will bring him out of his coma. My mama was a pianist and music teacher, you know."

"You know where the chapel is, don't you?"

"Yes."

"We came a wee bit early to see that the piano is moved where we want it. We'll see you there. I've already ordered the wheelchair for you. Come as soon as you can. Sometimes the chapel gets crowded when there's a concert," said Mrs. Cummings.

Emma watched as the two women left the room. Turning toward Papa, she noticed a twitch of an eyelash, or was that just her imagination? *No,* she thought, *nothing has changed.* She'd been hoping so long to see movement that now her imagination was tricking her. Just then the nurse arrived with the wheelchair.

As she helped lift him into the chair, she noticed how light and boney Papa had become. Nothing like his old hefty self. How she wished to feel his arm around her in a giant bear hug. She'd even make do with a pat on the arm. Struggling to control her feelings, she tucked a blanket around his waist, hips, and healthy leg; the one in the cast stretched out straight in front. "Well, we're all set. Let's head to the chapel to hear some music."

Emma maneuvered the ungainly chair out the door and started down the hall. It was slow going. Many other patients, along with nurses, were going in the same direction. Emma watched carefully not to run into anyone with Papa's outstretched leg. It was a challenge with so many people in the hallway going in the same direction. Greetings and laughter erupted as patients, visitors, and nurses joined others moving toward the chapel. Emma spoke to several patients she'd met over the weeks. She greeted the family members who stayed at the same hotel as her. They were like family and often shared meals and health concerns over afternoon tea.

❖

Emma watched Papa carefully for any sign of movement as the piano music flowed out over the audience. But as the concert continued she became lulled by the music into past musical memories. She recalled awaking in the mornings to the sound of her mama practicing. How she loved to lie in bed humming along with the tune her mama played. When Papa came into her room, he'd pick her up and help her into her long pink dressing gown. In his arms, they headed for the dining room where breakfast waited. Hugging him close, she would hum softly in his ear. That brought a smile to his face, along with a warm hug and kiss on the cheek. She loved those mornings.

Edmund, her brother, was always waiting for them at the dining table, anxious to dive into his breakfast. Emma smiled to herself as she pictured him. He was always so hungry and eager to start the day. They didn't have to wait long for Mama to arrive. Papa usually walked to the door of the music room, interrupting her practicing with a loud *humph*. At the table, she and Edmund listened as their parents exchanged plans for the day. They, of course, never spoke unless spoken to. Early in her life, Emma had learned that children were to be seen and not heard, a lesson she'd been forced to follow after the San Francisco earthquake, when she'd lost her voice and communicated using hand signals Caruso had taught her. What a delight it was to regain her voice after weeks without it. How wonderful if Papa could be jolted from his coma by the piano music they were hearing now.

Roused from her thoughts by the sound of clapping, Emma looked over at Papa. He sat strapped to the wheel chair with no apparent indication of a change in his posture. His head was slightly bent because she'd insisted they not tie his head to the back of the chair. She felt it was cruel to do so. Only the small pillows, one on each side of his head, and a rolled towel under his chin kept his head somewhat upright. His eyes, which had been closed all these many weeks, remained closed.

Emma's attention strayed as the next pianist walked to the piano centered in front of the chapel altar. It was the woman named Liz she'd just met that morning, the person who unnerved her by sending shivers through her body but also repulsed her because of her obviously once beautiful face, now scarred. In fact, Emma hadn't even wanted to shake her hand because it bore reddish scars similar to those on her face. She felt guilt and shame for how she felt.

As the music washed over the attentive audience, Emma, who held one of her papa's hands, suddenly felt a slight movement. Looking over at his face, she saw his eyelashes fluttering. Gasping, she turned completely toward him. Did she really feel his hand move? Did she see his lashes move? Intently she watched for more signs of awaking. Nothing. She squeezed his hand. No response. Calming herself, she slumped in her chair. Her imagination had once again played a trick on her. There hadn't been any movement in either his hand or his eyelashes.

After returning to the room, Emma helped settle Papa into bed. The nurse arrived to begin feeding him his daily nourishment. Emma never liked to watch the procedure. It was too ghastly, in her opinion. They fed him intravenously, a procedure still in its infancy, invented about sixty years before to help keep cholera patients alive. Watching the nurse put the giant needle into Papa's arm gave her the willies. She was always glad when the tube with the liquid containing nutrients was attached and she could watch the life-giving fluid moving into. his body. The needle part was the worst. His poor arms looked like a pincushion after weeks of intravenously feedings.

❦

Returning to his room after a brief lunch and brisk walk outside, Emma collided with a number of people gathered around Papa. Several doctors stood bedside, along with the two floor nurses. Off to one side, the hospital's Episcopal chaplain stood. Holding her breath, balancing on her toes, and glancing between people, she expected to see a white sheet over his head but there was none. Taking a breath, she asked, "What's going on?"

Turning toward her, Mayzie, the day nurse, smiled from cheek to cheek. "Your father has opened his eyes and moved his arms."

Emma's mouth opened into an astonished *O*, and she shoved her way through to stand by the bed. She grabbed his hand and squeezed, looking into Papa's wide-open blue eyes. She felt a weak pressure on her hand and saw him blink, as if he were trying to say, "Yes, I'm awake." Leaning forward, she threw her arms around him. "Oh, Papa, you've come back to me!" Emma choked as tears rolled down her cheeks.

Chapter 19

• • • • • • • •

Prognosis

All smiles, Emma watched as the doctors and nurses left the room, chatting among themselves. Only Chaplain Cuthbert remained. Approaching her, he said, "Let's give a prayer of thanks to the Almighty." She nodded and bowed her head.

"Lord, we thank you for this miracle You have performed today. All things are possible through You, Our Lord and Savior. May the healing process continue so that this, your servant, may be brought back to complete health. In Jesus' name, we thank you."

Crossing himself, Chaplin Cuthbert smiled. "You and your papa have been much blessed. I'm so happy for both of you. I'll leave you alone now, but don't hesitate to call on me if I can be of any help."

"You will continue to visit, won't you? Papa would like that."

"Yes, of course. I'll drop by daily on my rounds."

Smiling broadly, Emma turned to face Papa and squeezed his hand. "Oh, I'm so glad you're out of your coma. I've so much to tell you." Expecting a reply, she waited, studying his eyes, which she hadn't seen for months. She waited. Nothing. No gentle hand clasp, not even a twitch. Squeezing his hand three times, their special signal, she moved closer. "Papa, it's Emma. Can you hear me?"

She straightened and pulled her hand free to clutch her arms together, as if to give herself a hug. *What is wrong?* she wondered. She'd seen his eye movements just a few minutes-ago. She'd seen him move his fingers. Why wasn't he responding now? Turning toward the door, intending to finding the doctor, she collided with Wolfe.

"Zonks! Where are you off to in such a hurry?" he grunted.

"Finding the doctor," she responded piteously, jerking away from him. "Find the doctor."

Emma was babbling, not making any sense. Wolfe shook his head and moved aside, allowing Emma to run from the room.

"Dr. Springer!" she shouted, "Doctor, he's gone! Come quickly."

Dr. Springer and Emma rushed back into the room, sidestepping Wolfe. Papa's eyes stared straight ahead. The doctor waved his hand in front of the patient's face. Papa's eyes, although open, remained unseeing blue orbs. Emma's loud sobs echoed through the room. Wolfe stepped to her side and held her close.

Dr. Springer examined each eye and then held his stethoscope to Bruno's chest to check his heart and lungs. Lifting the nearest arm, he then released it, watching as it plunked back down on the bed with a thud. After closing Papa's eyelids, he stepped back and turned to Emma. "He's back in a comatose state.

Apparently, he came out of it briefly and then returned. I'm baffled why it happened. We're just going to have to wait and see. Perhaps he'll come out of it again and stay, but I can't promise you anything. It's totally in God's hands. Medically, we've done all that we can do."

Emma turned to Wolfe, burying her face in his shoulder. As she sobbed, she felt his arms enfold her, and he patted her back.

"It's not the end. Don't give up now. You never did when it looked like he hadn't survived the earthquake." Gently pulling her to face him, he asked, "Need my snotty hanky to dry those tears?"

With a weak smile, she nodded. He dabbed moisture from each eye with his large, bright blue cowboy handkerchief. Sniffling, she wiped her cheeks. "It's just so disheartening. He was conscious and now he's not. Why would God do that? Why would He give me hope and grab it away?"

Guiding her with a hand under her elbow, he led her into the hallway. "Let's take a walk."

Emma, numb from the latest twist of fate, allowed herself to be escorted out of the hospital, grateful that Wolfe held her hand as they walked. Her mind was blank, and she didn't want to talk. She was conscious of the warmth of his hand holding hers, their fingers intertwined. Suddenly she found herself back in New Braunfels, holding his hand while they ran through the cow pasture on Oma's old ranch. The breeze created by their running blew underneath her blouse, tickling her bare skin. How alive she'd felt! She and Wolfe had laughed as they raced along, jumping cow patties and dodging clumps of sod. The cows didn't raise their heads but continued chewing their cuds. It was late afternoon.

Only a bird or two that'd found refuge on a fence post gave them any notice. She could smell the sweet fresh air and see the cloudless blue sky. The warmth of the afternoon sun felt wonderful on her face.

"Careful, there's a step here," warned a male voice, jerking her from her musing. She felt Wolfe tighten his grasp as he guided her across the street. "How about stopping for a coffee?" he asked. Not waiting for an answer, he guided her into a small hamburger shop. He led her to an empty table and then walked to the counter to order coffee. Emma glanced out the window at the people walking by the shop.

Cars passed. People bustled along the sidewalk. A newspaper boy across the street yelled out the daily headlines to attract customers. A streetcar stopped and let a passenger off. *Life is going on for everyone but me*, she thought. Wolfe arrived, carrying two cups of steaming hot coffee. Placing one in front of her, he sat down opposite her with his own cup.

Before saying a word, he glanced out the window. Fingers around his cup handle, he raised it to his lips and took a sip of the dark, smoky liquid. Peeking over the edge of the cup, he tried to decipher the dear person sitting opposite him. Carefully replacing the cup on its saucer, he asked, "Shouldn't we start planning to take him home?"

Startled, Emma's hand bumped her cup, spilling some of the hot coffee on her fingers. She jerked back, causing more of her coffee to fill the saucer. "Oh, heck, look what I've done!" Tears appeared in her eyes.

Wolfe lifted her cup to place a doubled paper napkin in the saucer to soak up the spilled coffee. Placing the cup on the napkin, he commented, "It's just a spill. Don't worry. How's your hand? Should I ask for some ice?" She shook her head, and he reached across for the injured hand. Bending toward her, he kissed it. "Kissing makes it all better."

"Oh, Wolfe, you're so thoughtful. What would I do without you?"

"I hope you never have to find out. Now let's talk about moving your papa back home."

Emma nodded. Pressing her lips together, she looked toward the counter. On one of the seats sat the paperboy she'd noticed before. Noon was long gone, but it was obvious that the boy was waiting for something to eat. She watched as the owner turned from the grill with a plate holding a half-eaten hamburger. Placing it in front of the boy, he commented, "Eat up. It's the only leftover I have for you. Sorry, no chips."

Shaking her head, Emma wondered if she'd heard correctly. Was the boy given leftover food to eat? She swallowed. *How distasteful! But I guess if you were hungry and that's all you had, you'd eat.*

Turning back to her companion, she reached across the table for Wolfe's hand. "Yes, I think we must go ahead with our plans to take Papa back home."

Chapter 20

• • • • • • • •

Leaving Boise

Emma's plans to take Papa home immediately had to be postponed until after the fall cattle market when Wolfe and Juan discovered all the boxcars were rented out to ranchers shipping their cattle to the Denver stock market.

Emma continued her routines with Papa, reading to him and practicing her violin, in hopes of awakening him. She did spend time interviewing nurses who applied to make the trip to Santa Fe as part of a team caring for Papa. The number of applicants was dismally few. The doctor suggested a minimum of four, but Wolfe wanted six because of the length of the trip. He suggested that at Denver they could release two, saving some money.

As plans moved forward, Emma began to realize the tremendous expense involved in moving Papa home. *How can I afford the trip?* With both she and Wolfe gone from the store and Frederick, Wolfe's pa, the only one left to run the mercantile, profits had declined. And there was the matter of a note owed the bank. If not for Juan and Wolfe's salaries, they'd be in the red already.

Although she'd offered many times to work, both men were adamant that her job was to be at her papa's side.

The reality of the situation hit home soon after Wolfe returned from Donnelly. Mr. French laid him off. Winter approached. Most ranch hands were traveling south where the jobs were. Fortunately, an opportunity had opened with Mr. French's neighbor who ran sheep. Wolfe had no experience with sheep and was loath to take the job because he knew nothing herding. Furthermore, he didn't have a sheepdog. Sheep headers normally provided their own dogs. Wolfe told Emma about meeting a young Scotsman who'd arrived from the old country with two trained dogs, but because he was short of cash he had to sell one of the dogs to make it to the ranch where he'd been hired. The young herder still missed his four-footed companion, even though he'd kept the one.

❦

Distracted by her thoughts about finances, Emma turned into her papa's room. "I'm back. Hey—what do you think you're doing?" she shouted, rushing toward a burly man who was raising and lowering Papa's leg. "Stop that. He's in a coma."

The short, muscular man grinned. "Yes, I know. We must work these muscles so they don't atrophy." Holding out his hand, he said, "I'm Jack Best, a physical trainer. Father suggested I visit your papa and use my magic hands on him." Turning back to the patient, he lifted Papa's right leg, bending it at the knee and massaging the joint. He then started on the other knee.

Puzzled and a little miffed that she hadn't been consulted, Emma turned her attention to her father.

No change. Perhaps this physical contact would help—at least it couldn't hurt. Sinking down in the chair next to the bed, she watched as the trainer moved one joint after another, rubbing and kneading each part as he went. Finally, she asked, "How did you learn to massage like that? I've never seen anything like it."

As Jack Best worked, he answered, "As a young man I boxed in England, London to be exact. Part of the training is learning to treat sore and injured fellow boxers. When I came to this country, I couldn't box anymore. To keep my family fed, I became a janitor at the Children's Home Society of Idaho on Warm Springs Avenue. As you can imagine, children injure themselves frequently. I sorta stepped in as a father figure to ease their pain whenever they got hurt. It wasn't long before I had a new job with the school: chief miracle man. Soon the doctors in Boise began referring patients to me. Now I have a thriving business." Smiling, he turned to Emma as he covered her father with a sheet. "I'll come back tomorrow. Maybe he'll be ready to run a race with you when he wakes up. We'll work on that," winking at her.

"How much do you charge? I'm afraid I'm a little short right now."

"You owe nothing. It is all taken care of. Have a nice evening."

As Jack Best left the room, Juan entered. "Who was that?"

"A physical trainer who's going to work on getting Papa's body moving. How's the job of finding cowboys to break horses going?"

"Not good. Also, I received a notice from the college saying that I'd lose my place in the veterinary class if

I didn't register for the fall term. I hate to think of not finishing my degree."

Standing up to face him, Emma reached out for his hand. "You must go back. It's important that you graduate. The family expects it."

"I know, but I can't leave you here alone."

Shaking her head, Emma straightened to her full height but still having to look up at him. "Yes, you must. There's nothing you can do here. Besides, Wolfe's around."

Shrugging, he looked over at the prone figure on the bed. "I just pray that he'll wake up. I sent a telegram to Fritz and Maria concerning your need for money."

"I wish you hadn't. That's my responsibility, not yours."

"Well, I did. Fritz is telegramming money into your account. It may already be here. Also, while I was up in Donnelly, I was introduced to a Finnish woodcarver. Wolfe and I have arranged for him to send a few of his pieces down to Frederick to see if they might fill in the store's stock until he's able to make a buying trip to Mexico City. You know, those Finns are really excellent with wood. Most impressive."

Chapter 21

• • • • • • •

Problems

Walking the hospital halls became one of Emma's daily relaxations from the strain of bedside sitting. It wasn't long before she became acquainted with other patients and their visitors. Many who were not from Boise stayed at the same hotel as her. It didn't take long for her to learn the whereabouts of specific patients, especially the children.

She became attached to one such patient, nicknamed "Bunny Baby" because of the large protective bandages on each side of his head that looked like rabbit ears. Emma didn't know what had caused his injury but felt empathy for him. He received no visitors; he lay quietly in his prison-like bed responding to nothing, not even the nurses. Receiving permission to visit him, Emma popped in on him every opportunity she had. Having experienced abandonment, her maternal instinct drew her to him. As she talked to him she slowly dangled a small red yarn ball attached to a string above his head. Soon his eyes followed the ball, but there was no change in his facial expression. She told him children's stories and jokes her mama and papa had told her and her brother. After days of constant talking and teasing him with the yarn ball, she finally received a response. He grabbed for the ball. Soon Emma had Bunny Baby sitting up in his crib, playing with a larger yarn ball she'd made. The doctor and staff were delighted. He even began allowing her to feed him with a spoon, when before he'd only accept a bottle. That's when Emma overheard that the child had been abused by his mother before she disappeared. Touched by this knowledge, Emma's heart burst when Bunny Baby was well enough to leave the hospital; he'd be going to the orphanage just when he'd started calling her Mama! Her thoughts turned to Caruso and how he must have felt after seeing her off alone on the train to Santa Fe from Denver. No wonder he'd written so often to her!

A surprising frequent visitor to the hospital was Liz Wester, the pianist who'd given the concert just prior to Papa's awaking. Emma tried to avoid her as much as possible. She felt uneasy around her, and didn't understand why. But the woman seemed to kept popping in at the hospital to check on Papa. Wolfe met her on one of his visits; he confided that he thought she showed an unusual fascination for Papa. *But how could that be?* Emma wondered. He was just a comatose person. If she was forewarned of Liz's presence in the hospital, Emma usually made a point of going for a walk to avoid her. Once while she was practicing her violin, Liz entered the room and immediately blanched and fled. *Strange!*

Emma had heard that the Wester brother and sister were newly arrived Boise citizens, having only settled there in the last few years. The brother, an entrepreneur, first purchased an established saloon before starting a brewing and malting company that now supplied most of the state's beer. Recently he'd also opened a butcher and bakery shop.

The sister taught piano from their home and with some students rode horseback out to surrounding ranches to give lessons. Her students won prizes and awards at competitions all over the Pacific Northwest. They'd received recognition from as far away as Seattle. Why, wondered Emma, would Liz Wester, a teacher much sought after by those wishing to pursue professional musical careers, flee the room when she found her playing the violin?

❧

Emma sat across the table from Juan, who nervously cupped his hands around the half-filled mug in front of him. She wondered why he'd wanted to see her in such a hurry—something about news from New Mexico. "Don't keep me in suspense, Juan. What's the news you've received?"

He handed her the telegram he'd received and watched her face as she read. She slowly lowered the paper to the table and looked over at him. "How did this happen? The business was doing so well when I left," said Emma, shaking her head. "I built the one mercantile in Santa Fe into one of the major retail stores in the territory." Reaching across to grab Juan's hand, she said, "I guess Fred, Wolfe's pa, couldn't manage it all."

Shifting his feet as he pushed his mug into the center of the table, Juan looked directly at her. He tried not to flinch. "I've received other news too." Squirming in his seat, he continued. "Emma, you're months late with making payments on the store's loan. The bank's got to have its money within the month or they'll take over the business. You're broke."

The color drained from Emma's face as she bent her head and swallowed. Her finger in the mug's handle jerked, spilling coffee on the table top. "What about the house? Will I lose that too?"

Soberly, Juan shook his head. "No, it's part of my family's Spanish land grant. No one can touch it."

Absently, she pulled a napkin from the dispenser on the table and began mopping up the mess around her. "What about Fritz? Can he help?"

Looking straight at her, Juan quietly answered, "Things are tight right now on the ranch. Wool prices have bottomed out. Cattle too. There's just no extra money. I can't even go back to college—no money. They've had to let some of our sheepherders go, so I'm needed to fill in."

"How am I going to pay Papa's hospital bills?" crumpling the telegram into a ball before throwing it at him.

"Throwing things at me isn't going to solve your problem, Emma. Settle down and talk," said Juan.

"About what? That I'm broke and stuck up here with a comatose father?"

"You may not have any money, but I've saved just enough to get the two of us back. home. Wolfe is willing to stay here to care for your father. He's accepted a management job at Mr. French's dairy farm here in town. His new salary will allow him to cover your father's expenses as well as his own."

Emma looked over at her companion. What would she do without the two "adopted" brothers who took such good care of her? Too defeated to fight, she nodded her agreement. Returning to Santa Fe without her papa and leaving him alone here in Boise would be the hardest thing she'd ever done. There was no other choice left.

Chapter 22

• • • • • • •

A Grand Gesture

"You've lost your mind!" shouted Dillon, his index finger pointed at the person sitting rigidly at his desk listening to the outburst being played out in front of him. "You don't owe this family anything. You don't even know this man. Do you think you're your brother's keeper or something?"

"Calm down. Have a seat," said Jamie. "You didn't hear a word I said. In the last few weeks it has become apparent that this Bruno Roeder, for some reason or other, is very important to Liz. Why else would she visit him daily for hours on end? She even visits on Sundays after church where she openly prays for him during the time for prayers for the people. Some crevice has opened in her memory, and I mean to assist her down that avenue all I can."

"But why would you want a stranger in your home, along with a nursing staff to care for him? He's in a coma and has been for months—most likely he'll remain so for years. Do you want to take on that financial burden?" Pacing, Dillon stroked his chin with his right hand as he shook his head. "That was a foolish question to put to you. For years, you've nurtured a woman who doesn't know who she is."

Jamie stood suddenly, almost overturning his chair, and faced his friend. "That's enough. What I do is of no concern of yours. Liz's past memories are beginning to surface, just as the doctor in San Francisco said they would. I'm going to encourage her recovery, even if it means bringing this fellow Bruno here to recuperate. Whether he does or doesn't come out of the coma, so be it. I'm here for Liz. Accept it or not, I don't care. It's my life and my decision."

The two men stood staring at each other as the striking of the grandfather clock echoed in the silent room. Neither of them moved a muscle before Jamie turned to look out the window behind him. The view calmed his sudden eruption of anger toward his longtime friend, who'd been his companion through his search for the perfect location to quell his desire for wealth, love, and tranquility.

"Are you aware that you love her?" Dillon muttered. "I've never seen you so distracted by a woman or concerned with her welfare. What will you do if she suddenly remembers that's she married? What then?"

Turning dejectedly to his friend, Jamie confided in a hushed tone, "I think Bruno is her husband, but she hasn't recognized him yet. She's experiencing feelings but can't interpret them, but that will come. I want to be around for her when it happens, especially if he doesn't regain consciousness."

"Why do you suspect that he's her husband?"

"Did you ever look, really look, at Bruno's daughter, at her nose, mouth, and stature? They're the same as

Liz's. I'm surprised the daughter didn't see it or, for that matter, her friends. I think all of them were put off by Liz's scars from the San Francisco fire."

Dillon gave his friend's shoulder a nudge. "How long have you suspected this and said nothing?"

"What was there to say? When her father came out of his coma after hearing Liz play the piano, Emma failed to recognize her mother or even suspect. First Liz found it uncomfortable being around Bruno, and now she can't stay away from him. Liz doesn't understand it, nor does she want to talk about it. She wants him here in our house, close at hand." Inhaling, Jamie walked toward the fireplace, before turning toward Dillon, saying, "Yes, I have feelings for her. I always have since I rescued her. She's an exquisite jewel that the Lord dropped in my lap for safekeeping. I intend to do just that.

Chapter 23

• • • • • • •

Wolfe's Disclosure

"Wolfe, we're so glad you could join us for dinner," Jamie remarked as he held the front door open for him. "Let's go into the parlor and wait for Liz to join us." With Jamie leading the way, they walked down a wide hall covered by a deep-red figured woolen runner made by the Minnesota Woolen Mills that Wolfe recognized. The company was known for reusing donated wool to create new products for buyers. Many western families saved their cast-off woolen clothing, older rugs, and blankets for years in order to finance rugs such as this runner for their homes.

Jamie gestured to a chair close to the small ornate fireplace that glowed slightly but gave off enough heat to be felt. The room, like most parlors in wealthy Boise homes, was pocket size compared to the great rooms he was used to in New Mexico. It was furnished with a small sofa along a wall, two overstuffed chairs, and a high oval table with a lamp in front of the window.

Wolfe thought when he first received the invitation from Liz and Jamie that it was only a courtesy, so they could show him where they planned to house Bruno when he was moved from the hospital to their home. When he discovered they expected him to stay for dinner, he didn't know what to think. It wasn't Sunday, when everyone in Boise knew the Westers entertained many citizens, not just the bigwigs. For that reason and several others, he found himself in a quandary as to what to wear—a suit or just ordinary church clothing? He decided on church attire; however, he did splurge on a new white shirt to wear with his dark blue trousers. Wolfe was relieved to see Jamie was dressed much as he, in workday best, not a suit.

His legs and feet slightly apart, each hand resting on a knee, Wolfe looked over at Jamie, seated across from him, one calf across a knee. Just then Liz walked in, saying as she walked toward their guest, "Sorry I'm late."

After a quick touching of cheeks, Liz sat down, and the two men returned to their seats. Her head was cocked slightly to the side rather than facing him fully, and for just a moment Wolfe though she was Emma: same chin, nose, and forehead. Shaking his head to clear the vision, he refocused on the petite woman across from him. Could he be so hungry for the sight of Emma that his mind was playing tricks on him?

"I hear you've been more than a daily visitor to our hospital?" remarked Jamie.

Looking first at Jamie and then Liz, Wolfe nodded. "That's true. I've become quite interested in doctoring."

"Rumor has it that you're even going on house call with the doctor," said Liz.

"That's true," admitted Wolfe.

Hearing the pangs of hunger from his stomach and hoping the others hadn't, Jamie reached out and touched

Liz's elbow. "Shouldn't we be showing Wolfe the room so we can have supper?"

Glancing at both men, Liz stood. "Why don't we see the room now so we may discuss it while we eat."

After the trio visited Jamie's former office, now converted into a patient's room, they sat down to the meal Jamie had requested, a one-dish Irish stew the hoi polloi called Swiss steak, containing every kind of vegetable and chunks of beef, along with a side dish of mashed potatoes and freshly baked rolls.

Grabbing a roll, Jamie began to spread butter over both halves before he looked over at their guest. "Tell us a little about yourself and how you and Emma became acquainted."

After swallowing a bite, Wolfe took a sip of milk. With a sparkle in his eye, he chuckled. "We met when I fished her out of the river near New Braunfels, Texas, before the current could carry her downriver. She was visiting her Tanta's ranch with her oma—that's German for *grandma*. She was the only person around near my age, and we soon became best buddies when she visited the ranch."

"Why was she in Texas? I thought Emma lived in New Mexico?" Jamie asked as he passed the basket of rolls.

Taking a roll and passing the basket on to Liz, Wolfe then took his time dividing and buttering both pieces before answering. "Emma lost her family in the San Francisco earthquake. At first, she lived with her Uncle Fritz and Aunt Maria on a sheep ranch close to Santa Fe, but then her other uncle, Uncle Chris from Texas, went to court and got custody of Emma. That's how she ended up in Texas."

Suddenly Liz rose from the table without excusing herself and left the room. "Excuse me, I think I'd better see what's wrong," said Jamie, following his sister. Puzzled as to what he might have said to upset Liz, Wolfe sat back, absently glancing around the room. Thinking back to his earlier scrutiny of Liz, he recalled mistaking her for Emma. She had scarring on her face, perhaps from a fire. *Could there be a connection? Could Liz be Emma's lost mama? Could this be why Jamie and Liz offered to care for Bruno? Had they realized that Liz was Emma's mama and Bruno's wife?* He didn't have much time to contemplate before Jamie returned.

"Is Liz all right? I hope I didn't offend her in some way," Wolfe inquired, looking up at his host.

"No, no, it's not you. Liz has had amnesia since I rescued her from a building during the San Francisco earthquake. Every so often she gets glimpses of her past but never enough to shed light on her entire past. It's been disconcerting for her. She so wants to know who she is," Jamie explained as he rang for Dora. "You will have dessert with me, won't you? I think we have apple pie, my favorite."

There was silence as the men enjoyed large pieces of pie and cheese. After downing a glass of milk, Wolfe wiped his white mustache from his upper lip, commenting with a broad smile, "Hope this is French's product we're drinking."

Giving his guest a devilish grin, Jamie replied, "Is there any other?"

Relaxing in the newly arranged office on the second floor, the two men sighed contentedly before starting their discussion about Bruno's impending move. Both thought deeply about just how much each should reveal to the other. Each weighed the pros and cons of exposing all that they suspected concerning the women each had a connection with.

Finally, after studying the rough, red hands in his lap, Wolfe looked up at his host. "Why have you and Liz decided to take Bruno, a perfect stranger, into your home? It doesn't make sense, unless you know something Emma and I don't."

Jamie cleared his throat before answering. "Now wait a minute. Don't get all steamed up, but I think there may be some relationship between Liz and Bruno," he commented, holding up a hand when he saw his guest start to rise from his chair, looking indignant. "Let me explain. Liz visits Bruno daily and has for some time. She shows an unusual interest in him. She is also a survivor of the San Francisco earthquake. I think she lost her husband during the disaster in 1906."

"But," interrupted Wolfe, "She's your sister. You should know all about her."

"There's where you're wrong. She's not my sister. I just pulled her from a burning building and have been caring for her ever since, hoping she'll recover her memory. To eliminate the possibility of gossip, we tell everyone we're brother and sister."

Wolfe sat back down. Shaking his head, he stared at the man across from him. "I've noticed some similarities in Liz and Emma's facial features. I suppose it's possible that Bruno is Liz's husband, but how do we prove it?"

"We don't have to, but that's the reason I approved moving him here. Hopefully if she sees him daily, her memory will be jogged. Then we'll know. We just have to be patient until her powers of recall return."

"Shouldn't Emma be told?" Wolfe asked.

"Would you want to do that before we're certain?"

"It's too bad my pa only knew Bruno and not his wife. If he had, he could come up and identify Liz. Although he and Bruno were childhood playmates, after Bruno went to business school and my pa took up farming they didn't see much of each other."

"You never saw a picture of Emma's mother?"

"No, not that I know of. By the time Emma and I became acquainted, everyone thought Bruno, Ida, and Edmund, Emma's brother, had perished in the San Francisco earthquake. Because of some kind of family feud, the New Braunfels family kept no pictures."

"Edmund the brother was never found?"

"No, not that I know of. Well, I probably should be going. Milking cows is a before-sun-up job. Thanks for the supper." Shaking Jamie's hand, Wolfe said, "I think we both have our work cut out for us, you patiently waiting for Liz's memory to return and me for Bruno to recover so I can take him home. Good night."

Chapter 24

• • • • • • • •

Mishaps

Before Bruno arrived, Liz met with Dora and the rest of the newly hired staff, including the nurses, to go over her expectations and their schedules. Liz was a very detailed manager, even dictating the nurses' shifts and duties. The young nurses felt she was overstepping her authority since she wasn't a nurse, but since they were being well paid, they didn't complain except among themselves.

Because of the around-the-clock nursing, Dora hired her sister to help her with the preparation of meals and household tasks. Each nursing shift required two meals, doubling the amount of food preparation and serving. During the first several days Bruno was in residence, Dora could be heard muttering to herself, "Thank goodness our guest is unconscious and I don't have to feed him." It wasn't long, however, before she was heard saying aloud, "You wake up, you old fox, I'll gladly fix everything and anything your heart desires."

The entire household prayed for a miracle to bring Bruno out of his comatose condition. At Liz's request, the staff went about their tasks, making as much noise as they could, hoping it would induce him to join the world of the living. Everyone also was encouraged to visit the patient and talk to him for at least fifteen minutes a day. Many told jokes or funny stories that had the nurses in stitches.

Jamie frequently found himself walking around Bruno's room, discussing business in hopes the topic would awaken him. Although he never received any answers, Jamie found his time with Bruno relaxing. He guessed talking over his work problems, even if to a silent partner, was good for the soul. On occasion, he thought of his own father, wondering if they would have had a better relationship if he'd only taken the time to share his views and desires during his teen years.

Jack Best visited several days a week to use his magic fingers on Bruno. The small muscular Scot massaged and kneaded every part of the patient's torso with a special oil he applied to keep the skin soft and pliable. As he worked, he kept up a stream of conversation in his thick "old country" brogue, always ending with the promise, "Wake up, you lazy coot, and I'll give you a 'no nickel nothing with a thistle on the end'." Then he would laugh so uproariously that the sound could be heard throughout the house.

Liz continued giving piano lessons in the room adjacent to Bruno's. She practiced daily, beginning as early as five in the morning, or until Jamie rose to have breakfast.

Weeks passed with no indication of progress besides Bruno's increased restlessness, explained by his doctor as automatic responses and typical of patients in comas. The doctors arrived and left shaking their heads when

Liz inquired about the patient's progress. When Jack Best arrived to administer his magic manipulations, he seemed discouraged at times.

As the months passed, Liz and Jamie frequently sat silently at the supper table exchanging few words, lost in their own thoughts. Even when Wolfe or Dillon joined them for a meal, conversation was sparse; the men talked business, and Liz pretended to listen. Although unvoiced, hope for Bruno's recovery appeared remote.

※

"He's having a seizure," cried Jack Best as he rushed into the music room, interrupting Liz's practicing. "Help! I was massaging his shoulder. He's shaking. His tongue's back. Hurry. I can't hold him alone. The nurse is on a break. Help!" he shouted as he turned and ran from the room.

Jumping from the piano bench, Liz followed Jack from the room. Reaching Bruno's bedside, Liz quickly inserted a smooth flat stick between his tongue and the roof of his mouth so Bruno couldn't swallow his tongue. As his body contorted with the seizure, she spoke to Bruno. "It's all right. I'm here beside you. Hold on. This will be over soon."

Jack held fast to Bruno's contorting body, watching that he didn't fling himself onto the bed railings and get hurt. "I've never seen him have such a bad one."

"Everything's under control. We have to stay with him until the shaking stops. It was fortunate you were here when the seizure started and came and got me. Otherwise he might have swallowed his tongue and suffocated. Or worse yet thrown himself out of bed."

Looking concerned, Jack notice the shaking begin to subside. Bruno's body slumped on the bed like cooked oatmeal in a bowl. "Does this happen often?"

As she removed the stick from Bruno's mouth and put it aside, Liz's shoulders sagged. "He has these off and on, but thankfully not too frequently. Some are worse than others. This was a bad one. The doctor says they are caused by his concussion." Turning back to the bed, she added with a catch in her throat, "He may have brain damage."

The nurse appeared at the door just as Liz stopped speaking. Putting down her mug of coffee, she walked bedside. Looking up at Liz, the nurse nodded. "Sorry I took a break, Miss Liz, but I thought with Jack here everything would be okay."

"Don't worry. We never know when these seizures will occur, and you certainly aren't expected not to take breaks. It's fine," assured a weary Liz as she left the room.

※

After consulting with Dora as to which vegetables she required for the day's meals, basket in hand, Liz escaped from the house and retreated to the garden. She often found comfort in gathering food for their meals. Today she needed solace because of the plummeting agony of the sick room. As she unconsciously picked string beans and placed them in her basket, her thoughts turned to Bruno. Why, she wondered, did she feel this attraction to him? She didn't feel the same toward Jamie, who had rescued her from the fire in San Francisco and supported her ever since, even though she had no memory of her past. Why was she comfortable being around Bruno now that his daughter had gone back to New Mexico? In fact, when Emma, the daughter, was around, she felt anger toward the young woman. *Strange!*

With the basket full of green beans, parsnips, and lettuce, Liz turned to head back to the house just as the backdoor opened. Dora stuck her head out, shouting, "Your next student has arrived."

Hurrying, Liz held the basket tightly to avoid spilling the contents. Looking straight ahead toward the house, she suddenly caught her toe and fell head first on the brick path.

"Miss Liz, Miss Liz, are you okay?" shouted Dora as she ran toward the fallen figure. "Oh my, no! Help! Miss Liz's hurt." Dora knelt down, turning Liz over on her back. She was breathing, but her eyes were shut. "Speak to me," Dora encouraged. No response. She frantically turned toward the house, screaming, "Help! Help!" She cradled Liz's head in her hands and saw the beginning of an egg rising. "Please wake up, Liz."

❁

Jamie paced up and down the hall outside Liz's bedroom, waiting for Doctor King to emerge after his examination. He spun around when he heard the door open. "How is she?"

The doctor, black leather bag in hand, raised a finger to his lips, indicating a need for silence. Placing his bag on a side table, he motioned for Jamie to follow him to the end of the hall. "She's resting and aware of her surroundings. I've ordered the nurse to keep her awake for the next four hours so she doesn't lapse into a coma after the head trauma. She landed on the brick pretty hard and will have quite a large bump on her forehead. I've set her broken ankle. The next couple of hours will tell us how much damage, if any, the fall did to her brain."

"May I see her?" ask Jamie, combing his fingers through his hair and placing one hand in his pocket. Waiting for an answer, anxiety showed on his haggard face as he studied the doctor.

"I think it best that you let her rest for now. She's experienced a shock. Although we need to keep her awake, she'll do best with only the nurse around. I understand from talking with Jack Best that this morning wasn't an easy one for her. Mr. Bruno had a seizure, and she handled it alone because the nurse was off getting coffee. That couldn't have been easy and probably contributed to her being distracted when she was called back into the house. Oh, by the way, when did she start wanting to be called Ida? Is that her middle name?"

Chapter 25

• • • • • • •

Santa Fe, New Mexico

Following her Papa's custom, Emma stood looking at her reflection in the mirror. "Good morning, God. Thank you for another day." Turning her face from side to side, she scrutinized her seventeen-year-old features carefully for wrinkles, blotchiness, and pimples, especially the last break-out on her forehead, which for some reason she'd been having trouble with since returning from Idaho. "Well, old girl, you're not bad-looking now that you've hidden your acne." Turning back toward her bed, she began to dress for the day, but her thoughts strayed to her singleness and responsibilities. Most of her classmates were already married, many with toddlers or expecting. Would she ever have a family and normal life, she wondered? Shaking her head to vanquish those thoughts, she headed for the kitchen to make coffee before leaving for the mercantile.

Arriving at the shop, with Frederick nowhere in sight, she walked directly back to her office. Since returning from Boise several months ago, she'd managed to hold off the bank's threat of foreclosure for six months, but that was soon to end. Tomorrow she'd again meet with Frank Garcia, the bank manager, to see what could be worked out, but with no money to offer him, she knew what his answer would be. The sale of the Finnish wood carvings Juan sent from Idaho saved them initially, but she didn't have any prospect of money coming in any time soon.

"Morning, boss lady," distracted her from her gloomy thoughts. Looking up, she saw the smiling face of Wolfe's pa in the doorway. He was always cheerful, and she'd grown fond of the man since he began working for her papa several years ago, not only as a salesman but also as chief buyer.

"Any good news to share?" she asked, with little hope of a positive reply.

"Well, as a matter of fact I do." Fred grinned as he took a seat across from her. "I think I have an order for Mexican cobalt blue tile, a large order in fact, for the remodel of the old Exchange Hotel."

Emma straightened in her chair. "How much? Can you get what they want?"

He shifted to the edge of the chair, knees apart and fingers interlocked. He glanced first at the floor before looking up and grinning up at her. "We should make enough to pay off half the note, plus enough to pay expenses. I know exactly where to get the tile because I've dealt with the owner before. He's reliable. But ..."

They stared at each other for a moment before Emma asked, "How much?"

Shifting in his seat, Fred answered, "I'll need about one hundred dollars to manage the deal." Looking across at her, he added, "I know that's a lot, but if we can come up with it, we're certain to make a sizable profit. That would go a long way in paying off your debt, wouldn't it?"

Emma paced the office, trying to think of a way to come up with the needed sum. Shaking her head, she looked back at her hopeful manager and buyer. "We're flat broke," she stated. "I don't know where to turn. Fritz and Maria are in the same financial bind as us. Juan's family is strapped, and I wouldn't ask my Texas family for anything, even if I was starving."

"I won't say no to the people at the Exchange until we've exhausted all our possibilities. If I'm able to go get the tile, I know I could also bring back a load of furniture to refurbish our stock as well as replenish our spices that are in short supply. We desperately need vanilla and ground chili."

Emma plunked herself down at her desk with a sigh. "What a mess! Well, it can't be helped by sitting around here moping. Too bad the invitation to do a concert in Albuquerque isn't until next month. The promised twenty-five dollars, although not much, would have helped."

Fred looked up at her with a twinkle in his eye. "How about playing your violin out in front with a tin cup at your feet?"

"Oh, get along with you. You and Wolfe are both alike, never serious."

Getting up from his chair, he chuckled, gave her a wink, and walked out into the store.

❧

That evening, Emma stared at the lingering flames in the fireplace and enjoyed the smell of piñon that she'd so missed while in Idaho. Her thoughts turned to her absent family, especially her father. What was it he always said about adversity? Oh yes, things were always darkest before the dawn. Well, the present certainly represented gloom, and a little brightness would be welcome. As she looked around the room, she noticed the film of dust over the two end tables her mama brought with her from Texas. Her mother, if she were here, would chastise her for not dusting the only German heirlooms the family owned. Sighing she retrieved a cloth from the hall closet and began cleaning. After removing the dust from the top, she absentmindedly opened the drawer hitting her thumb on the wood above the opening. "Darn!" exploded from her lips as she lifted the hurt hand to her mouth to ease the pain.

Suddenly, out popped a hidden drawer. She jumped back. "What the …?" Stooping down for a closer look, she saw a fat cloth packet. She pulled it out, sat back on her haunches, and turned the sealed packet over and over before sticking her thumbnail into the cloth. Eagerly she fingered the pliant package, but it was too skillfully sewn to reveal its contents. Settling into a more comfortable nearby chair, Emma held the heavy packet in her hand, juggling it up and down to gauge its weight.

She set it on the end table while she retrieved scissors and a needle to undo the stitches. Returning, she set about the task of opening her find. Each stitch was so tiny that the scissors couldn't grasp between the threads, so she resorted to using the needle. It took ages to open a half inch. Exasperated and anxious to see what she'd found, she swore, "Darn! Double darn!"

"What's got you so upset?" came a voice from the doorway.

Not even looking up because she recognized Juan's voice, Emma held up the mysterious packet for him to see. "I can't open this darn cloth wrapping."

Entering the room, Juan knelt beside her and took the cloth object out of her hand. He slid his tiny knife from his pocket. "No problem. You've opened it enough that my knife will do the rest." And he sliced along one edge. "Whoa! There's sand in here." Shaking a little out into his hand; he gasped. "No. It's not sand—it's gold dust!" Wide eyed, he held his palm out for her to see.

"Gold! It can't be," replied Emma.

"Well, it is. Where did it come from?"

Looking blankly at Juan, she nodded toward the German table. Suddenly she moved to the drawer. "Could there be more?"

Sliding her hand in, Emma gasped. Recoiling back on her knees, grinning like a kid, she held up a second package.

In unison, they both shouted, "*Wow!*"

Tossing the second on the chair she'd been sitting in, Emma, still on her knees, waddled over to the second German table. Juan knelt beside her as she pulled out the drawer and began touching various spots on the wood, hoping for another hidden drawer. *Whish!* Another drawer appeared! Two packets, just like those she'd discovered in the first table, appeared. "How much do you suppose the gold is worth?" asked a jubilant Emma. "Enough to pay off the bank note and get the store stocked?"

"I have no idea," replied Juan. "You'll have to make a trip to the bank to find out."

❃

Emma, Juan, Fritz, and Maria sat around the supper table in Santa Fe, grinning and happily chatting. The comfortably cool thick adobe walls and shuttered windows that allowed only the late evening sunrays to flicker on the celebratory meal added to the festivities. They raised large glasses of fruit juice and cheered as they celebrated Emma's find, enough to pay off her entire bank note and more.

"Who would have thought your papa had planned so well and so secretively for your future, Emma? It's like a real Spanish folktale," laughed Aunt Maria at the end of the table.

"I'll bet Garcia was surprised out of his seat at your sudden wealth and ability to take care of the entire note. I know I was. That was the first real panned gold I've ever seen," remarked Juan.

Emma looked at the faces around the table before responding. "His eyes got as big as the tortillas we're eating at seeing the gold dust." Emma chuckled as she smeared honey on the tortilla she'd just taken from the basket. "And I bet mine got even bigger when he came back and informed me of the value of the gold dust." Looking smugly around, she continued with a downward glance. "I didn't take all the bags in to him. He doesn't need to know everything. Uncle Fritz, I'm wondering why your brother Chris didn't discover the gold years ago, when he came here after the earthquake to take me back to Texas?"

"He certainly failed to look in the right places. Who would have thought to look in the parlor? Most men would expect money to be hidden in an office safe.

Hiding things in furniture is a woman's thing," Juan joked with a sly smile. "Did you know about the secret hiding places, Uncle Fritz?"

Swallowing a bite, his uncle looked up. "I knew that some furniture brought from the old country had hidden compartments, but I didn't know Bruno and Ida had any. I'll bet God is looking down at us right now, chuckling at the joke He played on Chris years ago, as well the fantastic surprise He gave Emma. I've always imagined God up among the clouds sitting in front of a very large chessboard, with us humans as the game pieces, and checkmating us most of the time."

Maria's caramel eyes sparkled as she added, "My father, the priest, often said, 'God in His own time works miracles'."

Chapter 26

• • • • • • •

Awakening

"Mr. Jamie, may I come in?" asked Dora as she stepped into his office. "I'm sorry to disturb you."

Jamie looked up, beckoning her to enter. "What's up?"

"Well, sir, we are all confused now that Miss Liz is up and about. Since her accident, we never know what to call her. Some days she wants Liz and other days Ida. We never know which, and she gets angry no matter how hard we try. She's so different since her fall in the garden that we're all concerned. Charlie at the stable says she's riding almost every day and refuses to let him join her. He's worried, says the horse comes back all lathered up. She also appears confused at times, telling people she's not your sister. We're being quizzed by some townspeople about who she is."

"I'm aware of all this, Dora, and appreciate your coming to see me. Liz or Ida, whichever she wants to be called, experienced a real trauma with her fall last week. Dr. King says we just have to be patient with her until she adjusts to her new self. She's beginning to remember her past, after almost eight years of not knowing. Please understand and explain to the staff that we all must protect her as much as possible while she's adjusting and coming to terms with her previous self."

After Dora left, Jamie paced his office thinking about the advice he'd given Dora. He should practice what he preached, but could he be patient as well as understanding? Liz now realized that Bruno was more than a tickle under her skin; he was a living, breathing husband. She'd physically as well as mentally had distanced herself from him, her knight in shining armor, who'd saved her from the fire in San Francisco. He didn't know whether it was her conscience or a withdrawal on her part as she adjusted to acknowledging her marriage. Whichever, he was on the receiving end of a cold shoulder, and he didn't appreciate it. How he wished she would share her thoughts and feelings with him.

As Jamie walked past his old office on the main floor, he looked in the open doorway to see if all appeared normal. Liz/Ida sat next to the bed, her head resting next to Bruno's and holding his hand. One of the day nurses stood on the other side of the bed checking his heart and his breathing. Jamie hesitated before stepping into the room. Would he be welcomed he wondered? "How's our patient doing this morning?" he asked the nurse. Liz/Ida raised her head but offered no response to his question.

"Not so well, not well at all," answered the nurse.

Liz/Ida turned back to her husband, placed her face on his shoulder, and uttered a stifled cry. "Why? Why now, when I've just discovered who I am and who you are? It's not fair."

Jamie stood still, wanting with all his heart to go to her and throw his arms around her. It took all his strength to command his feet to remain anchored to the spot on which he stood. Beckoning to the nurse to step into the hall, he made his escape. "How is he really doing?" he asked, safely out of earshot of Liz/Ida.

Glancing toward the door, the nurse shook her head. "Not well, I'm afraid. His breathing's shallow, and he's having to struggle for every breath. His jerking has increased, and I'm afraid it's wearing him out."

"Shouldn't we get the doctor?"

"I think Miss Ida already sent Charlie for the doctor. They should be back very soon."

As Jamie reentered the sick room, he sensed at once a change in the atmosphere. Ida stood bent over Bruno, one ear near his mouth listening to his weak, barely audible whisper. Ida's arms encircled the boney shoulders over which she hung, listening intently. "Hold on, my love. We've found each other. Don't leave me now. I love you. I need you." She began kissing his lips. "Stay with me. I need you. I love you." She clung to him as tears streamed down her face.

Jamie turned away from the scene, wrapped in his own grief and unable to comfort the woman he'd grown so fond of over the past eight years. The nurse walked to the end of the bed and placed her hands on the iron footboard, ready to step in if she heard the death rattle.

Suddenly all was quiet. Ida climbed up onto the bed and lay outstretched beside her husband. The nurse glanced at her watch, noting the time for the death certificate. Jamie turned abruptly and bumped into the doctor rushing through the door.

✽

Jamie hung a swag from an apple tree wrapped with a wide black sash on the front door at the farm house just outside Boise, Idaho. The mourners, few in number, parked their motor vehicles, mostly Fords, in the circular driveway in front before making their way inside to partake of light refreshments after the short service at their church. Jamie stood at Ida's side as she greeted the arrivals. For Wolfe, it was a hurried affair because he would be leaving on the train east to escort the casket to Denver and then on down to Santa Fe. The men, including Jamie, wore black bands around the upper part of their suit sleeves. Ida, dressed all in black, including a veil that hid her face, wouldn't be making the trip. Dr. King had ruled the trip too strenuous given her health. Strangely, she hadn't fought the decree but meekly agreed.

After receiving the condolences of the guests, Ida withdrew to join Jamie and Dillon at the far end of the dining room while they partook of several of Dora's fancy sandwiches and tiny cakes and sipped punch. The few people gathered in the hallway, spoke in hushed tones among themselves while nibbling the finger foods provided, politely giving the bereaved time to recover from the simple but short service.

As Wolfe moved to Ida's side to say farewell, Jamie noticed Ida begin to teeter. Placing a hand under her elbow, he steadied her, enabling her to graciously receive Wolfe's leave-taking. "Do you want to sit down for a while or would you rather retire to your room?" Jamie asked. Feeling her slump slightly, he quickly provided support before she collapsed. Lifting her in his arms, he headed upstairs, followed by Dillon.

As Dora fussed over Ida in her bedroom, the two

men adjourned to Jamie's office. Sitting with glasses of ice water, the men stared at each other communicating, *Now what do we do?* Dillon was the first to speak, "What are you going to do about Ida now that she's lost her husband? She's all alone again and can no longer pretend to be your sister."

After placing his empty glass on the desk, Jamie crossed the room to stare out the window. After a brief silence, he turned back to face his friend. "I have no idea what to do or what's best to do. All I know is that I won't be throwing her out of the only home she's known for the past few years. Let people think what they want."

"Well, that's a first for you, who always has an answer for everything. Didn't you ever consider how you'd handle the custodial situation you placed yourself in when she recovered her memory?"

"Okay, remind me all you want. I know you thought I acted foolishly by bringing her to Idaho with me. You would have just cast her aside and gone on about your business, but I couldn't in good conscience do that."

Getting up from his seat, Dillon walked over to face his friend. "Yes, I didn't approve of your removing Ida from San Francisco, because there was a chance her family would have looked for her there, knowing it was the last place she'd been. I do understand your altruistic nature. You meant well, but now you must extract yourself from not only a public situation but also a very personal one. You do know you're in love with her, don't you?"

"Don't talk to me about my love. You're in love with her too."

"Touché!" responded Dillon, throwing his arms into the air.

Chapter 27

● ● ● ● ● ● ● ●

Surprises Galore

"She's what!" Emma shouted as she emerged from her office.

"That's what the telegram says. Your mama's traveling straight from Boise to New Braunfels, Texas. No explanation given," replied Wolfe from behind the counter.

Snatching the recently delivered telegram from his hand, Emma read it to confirm what he'd announced. "Why ever do you suppose she going there? She has no family left in Texas. She's not been back in almost thirty years. Does she hate me so much that she can't bring herself to come here?"

When Emma left Boise to return to New Mexico, she'd suspected that Liz was her mama. Why else would she had taken a special interest in her papa? Emma had expected some kind of communication from her to acknowledge their relationship soon after Jamie had written to confirm that indeed Liz was her mama, but none had been forthcoming.

"Maybe you should write Jamie to see if he has an explanation. He knows her better than anyone else now."

"She's my mother. Why wouldn't she write me to say she's not coming home? At least she owes me that much after I sent her a share of Papa's gold money."

"I don't know, but it's clear she's not stopping here on her way to Texas."

"Well, at least I know where I stand with this woman, and it certainly isn't as a beloved daughter!" exclaimed Emma before turning angrily toward her office. Settling back at her desk, she began sorting through bills but stopped midway to gaze into space. A sense of loss swept over her as she realized that with Papa's death she'd lost the only family member who really had cared about her. Well, except maybe her brother, Edmund. Leaning back in the chair, she pondered why she and her mama had never really been close. Her lack of musical talent seemed to be at the heart of the estrangement. As a toddler, she sang off key, couldn't whistle, and couldn't even hum to her mother's satisfaction. Her lack of ability to learn to read music provoked Mama. She'd frequently heard her say to Papa, "She's just lazy." Then there was her awkwardness, starting from the time she'd held her first baby spoon. Her mother always appeared embarrassed by her clumsiness even as she matured and became a little more coordinated. No, her mother had no affection for her. They'd never gotten along, which meant fighting over everything from playmates to clothing. It was probably wise that Ida went to Texas.

Saturday arrived. All the ranch people made their weekly, or monthly, trips to town. Customers crowded the mercantile now that their shelves were restocked with spices, bolts of fabric, and Cuban cigars. The town square in front of the Governor's Palace was filled with Navajos selling their jewelry, pottery, and blankets. During a lull at the store, Emma stepped out to visit her many Native American friends selling their crafts and to listen to the latest news from the reservation.

Emma walked down the row of blankets spread out on the floor under the overhang of the Governor's Palace displaying native crafts. She nodded to some and smiled to others. Halfway down the walk she stopped. "Lupe, you finished your blanket," she said to a grinning, round-faced woman.

"Yes, 'um. Gotta pay off the new stove you sold me."

"Don't worry about that. Is the stove working?"

"Oh yes. No more back pain from leaning over a pit fire."

"Glad to hear it," Emma remarked, continuing her walk.

At one blanket, she stopped to glance at the display of silver rings. She still wore and treasured the turquoise one her brother had given her on her tenth birthday.

After finding the stash of hidden gold, she'd begun the practice of purchasing family jewelry from her Navajo friends when they were financially strapped and holding the prized family treasures until they could buy them back from her. Few knew of her pawnbroker business except Wolfe, who teased her about it constantly.

❧

On one Saturday evening, as all the family sat around Emma's dining table sharing gossip and news, Wolfe made the surprise announcement that he'd been accepted at the Colorado Medical School in Denver starting in the fall. Surprised and a little hurt, Emma asked, "When did you decide you wanted to be a doctor? This is the first I've heard of it."

Smiling as he smoothed down his unruly golden hair, he replied, "When I was in Boise watching the doctors care for Bruno, I thought what a wonderful gift it was to help sick people recover. During those months after you'd returned here and I remained in Boise with Bruno, when I could, I started traveling around with Dr. King as he visited patients. Those hours with him really piqued my interest. With his help and encouragement, I applied to the medical school, not really expecting to be accepted, but the letter came a couple of days ago. The school in Denver just opened, so if I work hard, I'll be in one of the first graduating classes." Looking straight at Emma, he added, "I hope you're happy for me?"

"Of course, I'm happy for you, just very surprised. I'm going to really miss you. The customers will too. You're helpful and cheerful, even with difficult people like my uncle." Emma grinned mischievously at Fritz, who nudged her foot under the table.

As Maria got up from the table she frowned slightly, "Guess you're going to be hiring new help. Wolfe will be hard to replace."

"Yes, I know, but I don't want to think about that right now. Let's just celebrate his good news. I know that Papa up in heaven is joyful at the part he played in Wolfe's decision."

Turning to Juan, Wolfe asked, "You're majoring in animal husbandry, aren't you? Aren't you about finished with your program?"

Nodding, Juan looked around the table and smiled.

"I graduate in a few weeks. I hope you all come down to graduation."

Returning to the table, Maria slapped Juan on the back. "We'll be there with your parents. All of us are so proud of you for being our first college graduate."

"Yes, we're all so proud of you. What do you plan to do after graduation?" Emma asked.

Laughter erupted all around the table as Maria and Fritz said in unison, "Create woolier and meatier sheep for the ranch."

"What about a few less obstinate mules too?" added Wolfe, getting into the swing of the family jokes. "You'll need obedient stock to pull the wagons of wool to market."

"No," replied Juan, getting up from the table and nudging Wolfe on the shoulder. "I'm going to purchase some of the trucks Henry Ford's manufacturing to do that."

"And I guess I'm going to Texas to learn from Uncle Chris the fine art of buying and selling wool," Emma added.

"No you don't—that's my territory," declared Fred. "My son may be going off to medical school, but I'm staying right here. I love my job."

Chapter 28

• • • • • • • •

Disappearance

After seeing Ida off on the train to Denver, Jamie and Dillon parted, heading back to their respective homes. Jamie was not happy at parting so soon after Ida had recovered her memory. He was concerned how knowing and accepting her past life might affect her coming to terms with her future.

As he walked from the train station, his entire body rebelled at facing life without Liz. In an attempt to control himself, he turned his thoughts to the many decisions waiting for him at his office. His butcher shop was running smoothly, but the adjoining bakery needed a new baker, preferably someone French who knew how to make the pastries demanded by the gourmet tastes of Boise's patrons. Reaching his office, Jamie sat behind his desk staring at her picture. How was he going to keep going without her? His heart ached.

Without Liz around the house in the evenings, Jamie found that thoughts of his "lady" invaded his mind, pushing out other reflections. Sometimes he'd awaken at night to the sound of piano music, but when he tiptoed down to the music room, he'd find no one at the piano. Several times as he left for work, he saw a specter standing in the house garden that disappeared when he called out a greeting. He lost all interest in his orchard, the garden, and even horseback riding.

In desperation, he ended up locking the music room door, hiding the key, and ordering Dora not to enter. As for Ida's suite of rooms, he'd closed them off, blocking further use of them. Using work in town as an excuse, he spent as little time as possible at home and never entered his office.

Dora and her sister moved the office back downstairs to its original location, but the vision of the hospital bed with Bruno in it and Ida seated beside him haunted Jamie when he thought of using the room as an office. He considered moving it back upstairs but hesitated placing more work on Dora. She, too, was adjusting to an empty house.

He stopped having the large Sunday dinner gatherings. Dillon joined him occasionally for a Sunday dinner, but now that it was only the two of them, conversation was stilted and limited. Without Liz, his desire to socialize was gone.

Several weeks after Ida's departure, Dillon burst into Jamie's warehouse office. "Have you heard from her?"

Looking up at his friend, who appeared disheveled, Jamie frowned. "What do you mean have I heard from her?"

"I just learned that Ida never reached New Braunfels. No one has seen her."

Shaking his head, Jamie stood up slowly. "I knew one of us should have escorted her to Texas. Why was I so stupid?" Waving a hand at Dillon, he added, "Yes, yes, I know you offered when I was too, too disheartened to go. You were right, you were right—one of us should have gone with her." Pacing behind his desk, hands in his pant pockets, he muttered, "Now what do we do?"

Slapping his hat on the desk in front of him, Dillon answered, "I know what you must do. Use your business contacts in Denver to see if anyone has seen her. Surely one of your many customers would have noticed a beautiful woman like Ida about town alone."

"Yes, you're right. I should also wire Emma to see if she's seen or heard from her mother. Perhaps Ida changed her mind and went to Santa Fe."

"Worse still, with all the money she carried something could have happened to her," replied Dillon as his friend grabbed his hat and headed for the door.

"Don't even think that. I'm sending a wire to Santa Fe," came the answer from the receding back.

❈

Jamie's wait for answers to his many telegrams about Ida's whereabouts was excruciating. Dillon kept him company at the brewery office because it was near the telegraph office. He ordered milk, coffee, and food from a restaurant down the street, but neither of them had much of an appetite. The food went untouched most of the time.

As answers to his telegrams arrived, Jamie crumpled

them and threw them in the wastebasket, letting loose a groan with each one of them. The telegram from Santa Fe was the most disheartening: no Ida.

"I wish I could go to Denver, but I can't. I've just promised a neighbor I'd help him during calving," Dillon announced as he left Jamie's office.

Not looking up, Jamie nodded. "I understand. I'm not sure I can get away right now either. And if she doesn't want to be found, what chance do we have of finding her?"

Discouraged, Jamie left his horse in the barn and headed toward the house. His mind was reeling with the thoughts of his Ida alone in Denver. Perhaps she'd had a lapse of memory or the amnesia had returned on the train. He was going to Denver. To hell with business.

As he approached the back door, Jamie collided with Jack Best. "Sorry, Jack. What brings you out here?"

"Been waiting for you but was about to give up. Have you any news?"

Shaking his head, Jamie proceeded into the kitchen, followed by Jack. "Come on into the parlor where we can talk," Jamie said with a sweep of his hand. "Dora, could you bring us some tea?"

"That won't be necessary," croaked Jack. "I can't stay long."

After they sat, Jamie looked at Jack expectedly. "What's on your mind?"

Before speaking Jack cleared his throat. "I know Liz, I mean Ida, hasn't shown up in Texas. I guess everyone in Boise knows that by now. Anyway, I've been replaying in my mind some of the conversations she had with Bruno, thinking maybe there might be a clue as to where she'd head." He glanced at the man in front of him before continuing. "She thanked him, you know Bruno, repeatedly for rescuing her from spinsterhood. Said she never thought he'd choose her as his wife over Helga, who was prettier than she. As I recall, Ida's former boyfriend married Helga rather than Ida. Made her feel rejected and unlovable, she said. Some days she spoke about the loss of her parents and siblings. She blamed herself for their deaths. Working at the orphanage had helped her forget about her lost family. She even begged him, Bruno, to live because she didn't know how she'd cope with being all alone."

Jack fell silent after his revelation. Only the ticking of the grandfather clock was heard. Jamie sat, legs apart, forearms resting on the chair arms, staring at his guest. "Does that give you some ideas? Or at least help? I know it's all mixed up, but that's how she was thinking."

Jamie stood and approached Jack with an outstretched hand. "Thank you. Thank you so much. I'll stay in touch." He offered his visitor a handshake and saw him to the door. Going into his office, Jamie collapsed in his chair behind his desk. Sitting back, he looked up at the ceiling for a few seconds before ringing for Dora.

"Pack a bag for me, Dora. I'm going to Denver on the late train."

Chapter 29

• • • • • • • •

Denver 1912

After heaving his bag into the rack above his seat, Jamie settled down next to the window. He tipped his hat to shield his eyes, crossed his arms, and settled down to sleep. The passenger car was half empty as it slowly moved out of the Boise station.

"Tickets, please. Have your tickets ready," announced the uniformed conductor walking down the aisle and stopping at occupied seats to punch tickets.

Jamie roused himself to retrieve his ticket from his breast pocket. After it was handed back to him, he glanced around and saw that several rows of seats in front of and behind him were vacant. Grunting, he returned to his sleeping position and closed his eyes. The gentle sway of the train soothed him into a welcome slumber, one that had escaped him since Ida's departure.

Waking to the sound of the conductor hurrying by, he sat up. The darkness outside had been replaced by faint light. He'd slept through the night for the first time since Liz's departure. Stroking his chin, he realized he needed a shave. Reaching above, he lowered his bag to his seat and, after fumbling around, found the small bag containing his shaving equipment. He headed for the men's room toward the end of the car.

Refreshed after a wash and shave, Jamie started down the aisle toward his seat. Glancing ahead, he shook his head thinking he'd recognized a hat. As he repacked his shaving gear, he looked back again to see the hat, but it wasn't there. He muttered to himself, "You're seeing things, old man. You're too young to be losing your mind."

Taking his seat, Jamie tried to concentrate on the passing scenery, but Liz, now Ida's, smiling face traveled along, interposed between the glass and the view. He drank in each familiar feature, longing to touch the soft warm cheeks, the delicate lips, the enticing ears and yes, even the scares on the side of her face. "Why, why did you let her leave you?" he muttered to himself. *Heck*, he reminded himself, *now I must think of her as Ida, not Liz, which I preferred.*

As the hours passed, he sat alone with his thoughts, unaware of everything around him. He chastised himself for taking her for granted, for refusing to admit his love, for not telling her how he felt. He prayed that he could find her before it was too late. He asked the Lord to keep her out of danger and away from all harm. As time passed, he hung his head, letting the tears form so he could mop them up with his "snotty" handkerchief, as Ida always said; that brought a smile to his face. How he missed her little jokes and funny sayings.

"Denver coming up! Next stop, Denver," called the conductor as he walked through the car.

Jamie stood up to retrieve his bag from above. At the same time he glanced down the aisle at the other passengers. "*No*, it can't be!" he told himself. There, near the end of the car where people exited, stood Dillon. Ducking down quickly beside his bag on the seat, Jamie was in a quandary. What made him not want to be seen by his long-time friend?

❧

In 1912 Denver was home to several hotels. The Albany, built in 1885, was famous for hosting the Democratic Convention in 1908, and the Oxford, built in 1891, was within a block of the train station. Jamie followed Dillon until he entered the Oxford and then proceeded farther up to the Brown Palace Hotel, opened in 1892, a more lavish establishment built in a triangular shape where he often stayed when doing business in Denver. Although not as regular a customer nor as famous as Molly Brown, Jamie was well enough known by the staff to be given superior accommodations.

On the train ride from Boise, Jamie had devised a plan of likely places to look for Ida: music halls, theaters, and saloons topped his list. His first visit was to the hotel's famous Cruise Room with a bar at the far end; he inquired if anyone had seen her. From there he widened his search to include public and private entertainment establishments. Nothing!

Despondent after several days of walking the streets of Denver, Jamie wondered if Dillon was having any better luck than him. Or had his friend arrived in town knowing where Ida was? Could she have contacted Dillon without him sharing the information with him? Perhaps that explained his trip so soon after saying he couldn't travel.

That night, torn by doubts, Jamie tossed and turned as he tried to get some sleep. Giving up around four in the morning, he dressed and went down to the restaurant for a mug of warm milk. Sipping it, he decided to throw caution to wind and contact Dillon.

The walk down to the Oxford dampened Jamie's suspicions, so when he entered the hotel and encountered Dillon in the foyer, there wasn't an instant explosive exchange.

"Jamie, when did you arrive?" asked Dillon, flabbergasted at seeing his friend.

He clenched his fists before replying. "I should ask you the same. I thought you were too busy to travel," Jamie countered in a belligerent tone.

"You claimed to be too busy too," snarled Dillon, bracing himself as if ready for a fight.

Standing in the hotel lobby, they stared at each other defiantly, each trying to measure the other's intent. The few passing people gave them a wide berth and questioning looks. The hostility between them heightened as the seconds passed without a word being exchanged.

Turning, Jamie said over his shoulder, "I haven't found her, but I take it you've known all along where she is." Opening the double entry door, he turned back. "I'm through with your charade. I'm finished. I've known all along you wanted her, even though you disapproved of my bringing her along. What did you two plan, a rendezvous in Denver? I'm finished with you both." With that he walked out and, with determination, turned in the direction of his hotel.

Dillon stood staring after his friend, completely puzzled. What had just happened? Why did Jamie think he knew Liz's whereabouts? How did he come to that conclusion? Shaking his head, he walked toward Civic Center Park to begin his search for the lady he hoped to persuade to marry him.

Chapter 30

• • • • • • • •

Santa Fe to Denver

After unlocking the store, Emma, followed by Wolfe, entered the cool, dark store, with its stale odor from being closed all night. Emma watched Wolfe crack a few windows and start the overhead fans while she prepared the cash register for business. Sweeping her hand over the smooth wooden counter, she sighed as she recalled jumping from it into her papa's waiting arms, trusting that he would catch her. Had she been three at the time? Next to the cash register was the enclosed glass candy display case. Even now, at her age, she craved a peppermint stick midafternoon, for energy, mind you. She stood at the counter, apprehensively waiting for Wolfe to join her so they could start the conversation they both knew had to be voiced. Each hesitated over bringing up the topic of Wolfe's pending departure to start medical school. Neither looked forward to the separation, each for different reasons.

On Wolfe's advice, Emma hired Antonio Garcia to fill the vacancy at the store. Antonio, a fatherly Spaniard, had years of merchandising experience in Taos but wished to move closer to his elderly parents in Santa Fe. Antonio's children were all grown, and his wife, Anna, was willing to move closer to her own family. Emma's problem of running the mercantile alone seemed solved. However, a feeling of great loss remained.

She had yet to face the idea that when Wolfe's pa traveled on business, which he did frequently, she'd be completely alone at work and at home. Juan, of course, would visit frequently but there would still be long periods of loneliness. Emma smiled to herself as she thought of Juan, who everyone thought would return to work for Kittie after helping his family through their financial problems on the ranch. It had been less than six months after their return to New Mexico that he'd confessed that he'd discovered that Kitty wasn't interested in his husbandry knowledge or willing to share her methods of stock development. She only wanted him to break horses so they could be sold. Often as many as 156 horses had to be broken every two weeks to meet her buyers' needs, and that meant continually breaking broncs. The cowboys on Kitty's Diamond Ranch were known as the best riders west of the Mississippi; several good enough to be hired by Buffalo Bill's Wild West Show.

Emma hadn't planned to go with Wolfe when he left for Denver. She thought the separation would be easier to take if she remained at home. But Jamie's letter arrived, reporting he and Dillon had traced her mama to Denver where her trail went cold. She'd disappeared off the train and into the streets of the unknown. Emma's sense of family loyalty dictated she must travel to Denver and try to locate Mama

Emma having discovered recently that she possessed a natural instinct of sorts, thought she might be able use her gift to locate her mother even though there hadn't been any vibrations between them since her leaving Boise. Recalling her physical reaction to the women she now knew was her mama, Emma realized her feelings while around Liz in Idaho signaled the familial connection between them.

"I'm glad you're going to Denver to search for your mother," Wolfe commented. "But you know I won't have any time to help you. I have to find housing and meet with my advisor before the start of school."

Moving behind the counter, Emma picked up an invoice, glancing at it before replying. "I know you'll be busy, but won't traveling together up there be fun, before we have to say our good-byes until Christmas?"

Grinning, Wolfe gave Emma a seductive look. "Yes, it will be wonderful to have you all to myself, with no distractions."

❧

Arriving in Denver, Emma and Wolfe chose to stay at the Oxford Hotel, a hotel familiar to Emma because it's where she and Juan stayed as they passed through Denver on their way to Idaho. The wooden floor showed more scuff marks, the arms of the chairs were threadbare, but the man behind the desk welcoming. They were given rooms on different floors as was the custom. Propriety had to be maintained.

Denver had grown since Emma was there last. The change in odor on the streets struck her first. The pungent smell of horseflesh had been replaced by gas fumes from the automobiles noisily bumping along the streets, making crossing them hazardous. Emma was almost run over once. Most of the open markets had retreated inside, probably because of the ghastly street smells. The store where Emma had worked was still operating. The manager even offered her old job back. As Emma scoured the busy streets, marveling at all the changes and checking with merchants that the store in Santa Fe did business with, Wolfe headed out in search of housing close to the medical school. Each evening they met over dinner at the hotel to discuss their day.

"Any success?"

"No," became Emma's standard reply. "How about you?"

Wolfe would shake his head at her question, look down at his plate, and grumble, "Single rooms are too expensive, and I'm not sure I like the idea of sharing."

"Isn't the school helping at all?"

"Sure. They have many listings, but most are too far away. I was hoping for a place close enough I could walk, not ride a bus. Tomorrow I'm going to check a room that's just been listed. The college won't vouch for it because this is a first-time listing."

After swallowing a bite, Emma replied with a twinkle in her eye, "Maybe you should use your charm on the landladies to get the deal you want."

"The landladies I've been meeting are stone faced, hard business people who are trying to make a living off struggling students. Charm has nothing to do with it."

"Boy, have you turned into a pessimist."

"You would, too, if you'd been turned down as many times as I have. Let's talk about your search. How's it going?"

"I'm still optimistic that I'll find Mama. I feel she's close."

Holding a bite midway to his mouth, he ventured, "Have you had another one of your premonitions?"

Holding his gaze, she whispered, "Yes."

"Well?"

"She seems distance because there's something in the way. I don't understand what or who."

Finally placing the bite in his mouth, Wolfe chewed slowing, frowning as he shifted his gaze from Emma to the people sitting at the next table. Why did she always unbalance him with her ability to foresee future happenings, a quirk he'd learned about after she returned home from Idaho, or was it that she'd just decided to reveal it to him? It was uncanny how often her predictions turned out to be correct. He wondered what Juan thought about them?

Placing his folded napkin alongside his plate, Wolfe leaned back in his chair, scrutinizing the serious face across from him. "How do you feel about your mother now? You've always said your brother Edmund was her favorite and that she disapproved of you."

Leaning over the table toward Wolfe, Emma cast her eyes around the empty dishes in front of her. Looking up, she replied, "I'm working hard at sorting out in my own mind how I really feel. For years Papa was my whole world. As a little girl, I even dreamed of marrying him. My love for him was so intense there were times I dreamed of just Edmund, Papa, and me being a family." Catching Wolfe's eye, she tried to read how he'd taken her statement, but seeing no reaction, she continued. "I thought Mama was distant and dispassionate toward me when I was a child, but now, looking back, I think I was drawn toward Papa because he made a fuss over me and Mama didn't. Mama disciplined me, tried to teach me things that I needed to learn. I see that now."

"Are you saying you want to make amends?"

"Yes, I think I am."

Looking around the hotel dining room, where they were the only couple left, Wolfe pushed his chair back from the table, rose, and went around to Emma's chair to pull it back from the table so she could stand. "I don't know about you, but I'm ready to call it a night. Morning will come all too soon for me."

"Yes. Me too," agreed Emma, walking ahead of him toward the hotel lobby. "I also have a new novel I'd like to start before going to bed."

After leaving her friend for the night, Emma arrived at her room, feeling unsettled. Why had she shared her premonition about Mama with Wolfe? If she was wrong, she'd be embarrassed. She didn't want to appear foolish in Wolfe's eyes, of all people.

Before pulling the shade down over the window in her room, she glanced down at the street, lit up by the street lights revealing strolling couples, men rushing home, and horse-drawn carriages and motor cars. So busy, and so unlike Santa Fe at nighttime.

About to turn from the window, Emma suddenly caught sight of a lone figure walking below. "I recognize that man!" she exclaimed aloud. She leaned her forehead against the window for a better look. Excitedly she turned from the window, grabbed her purse, and ran out into the hall.

Chapter 31

• • • • • • •

The Encounter

"Emma!" exclaimed Dillon as he saw her running toward him from the hotel stairway. "You're in Denver?"

"Yes, of course! Have you found Mama?"

Dillon looked down into her sparkling bluish-green eyes and knew he couldn't keep his secret from her. "Yes, I found her today, as a matter of fact. Come and have dinner with me," he invited. "I haven't eaten since breakfast!"

"Of course I'll join you." As they walked together toward the dining room, she chatted. "Wolfe's in Denver, too, staying here until he finds a room to rent while he attends medical school. Will this table do? You look starved. I want to hear about Mama."

Emma waited impatiently as Dillon ordered his medium-well-done steak and insisted that she at least have a cup of tea. Sitting on the edge of her seat, she restrained herself from interrupting him when he started a conversation with the waitress about what vegetables were available that evening. As the serving girl turned from the table, Emma blurted out, "Well, come on! Tell me! Where's Mama?"

Giving her a beguiling smile, Dillon confided, "I've been visiting different city parks daily ever since arriving in Denver in the hopes of spotting her. Today I went back to my favorite, one I knew would be one your mother probably loved too. Civic Center Park is not far from here and near enough to all Denver's cultural events to allow a person to walk to any one of them without much effort."

"Okay," replied Emma excitedly. "But tell me about seeing Mama. Stop keeping me in 'suspenders,' as my papa used to say."

"Oh, come on, Emma. Let me get little enjoyment out of telling my story!" he teased as his dinner was placed in front of him.

Frustrated, Emma hurriedly placed her finger in her cup's handle, almost spilling tea into the saucer. "See what you've made me do," she said to Dillon gleefully.

"While I'm eating, tell me about Wolfe's decision to attend medical school."

Relaxing, Emma settled back in her chair and, with the most engaging of smiles, began sharing Wolfe's recent decision. "You'll remember I had to leave him in charge of Papa's legal care when I left to return to Santa Fe to take over the business. Well, he spent a lot of time with Papa's doctors and became interested in how they heal people. He'd never known anything but farming while he was growing up in Texas, and when he and his pa moved to New Mexico with us, he worked in merchandising for my papa. During his time in Boise, he discovered he really liked to cure people. So, he came to the decision to attend medical school."

Dillon chewed, nodded, and sipped his coffee as he listened to Emma. After his last bite, he took a big swallow of coffee before speaking. "I finally spotted your mama today and followed her to where I think she's living, or I hope she is." He smiled. His persistence in checking that park today had paid off; late in the afternoon he'd sighted Liz sauntering along a park path, enjoying the many blooming flowers. When she found a bench on which to rest, he'd been hesitant as to whether to approach her or keep his distance. He'd decided on the latter, so he found a bench nearby and gazed at the beauty of the woman he'd fallen in love with and had not seen in several weeks.

"Didn't you identify yourself?"

"No. I didn't know what to do. Besides, did you know that Jamie is also in town looking for her?"

"No, I didn't. Where is he?" asked Emma, looking around expecting to see him.

Moving his mug aside, Dillon cleared his throat. "We're no longer friends. We argued over your mama."

"Argued? How so?"

"Jamie accused me of knowing her whereabouts when I arrived here, which wasn't true. He thinks, and is correct in thinking, that I have feelings for your mama. So you see, we've had a falling out. He sees us as rivals."

Emma couldn't contain the smile that crept across her face. "Are you two just figuring that out? I recognized right from the day we met that you both had feelings for Liz."

Shyly shifting his eyes downward, Dillon softly replied, "Yes, well, neither one of us wanted to admit it to the other because of her amnesia. We were so concerned about her, each in our own way, that we concealed our feelings."

"Will you let him know that you've found her?"

Raising his head to meet her gaze, Dillon grunted. "We may have exchanged words, but I'm no tumbling sagebrush when it comes to friendship. Yes, I'll tell him."

"Glad to hear it. I'm anxious to start making amends for the past with Mama or at least see if there's a chance that we can. I know it won't be easy because of the past animosity between us from my childhood," said Emma.

"You may be surprised how she feels toward you," commented Dillon, searching the young face opposite him. "Children often attribute to their parents, especially the parent of the same sex, erroneous standards of their attitude toward them. I know in my case I felt my father disliked me because of his infrequent praise and apparent disapproval. It was only after leaving home and being on my own I began to understand that his stinginess with praise wasn't because he didn't take pride in my accomplishment but because he was preparing me for living in the real world, where compliments are seldom voiced and criticism frequent."

Emma reached across the table to grasp her friend's hand and squeeze it. "Thank you for that insight. I will keep it in mind as I try to heal the bond between Mama and me."

As the two parted for the night in the lobby, they set eight o'clock as their meeting time to head out to locate Mama.

Chapter 32

• • • • • • • •

A New Surprise

The "short walk" described by Dillon to Ida's the night before turned out to be quite a trek from the hotel. Emma stood facing the house, contemplating their approach to what appeared to be a mansion. With a quizzical look, She turned to Dillon. "Are you certain you saw Mother enter this house?"

"Yes, I'm certain."

"But how can she afford such an elegant house? She didn't inherit that much from Papa's gold stash!"

"Well, there's no sense standing here and wondering. Let's go up and see."

"I don't know that I can face her. What if she refuses to see me?"

"You will never know by standing here and debating. Remember, I'm right here with you, no matter what happens. No cold feet allowed." Taking Emma's hand, Dillon gently guided her toward the front entrance.

After they knocked, the ten-foot door opened to reveal a matronly woman dressed in a gray dress adorned by a white lacy collar. "Yes? Can I help you?"

Emma hesitated and shifted her feet. She glanced up at Dillon for help. Still holding her hand, he smiled. "Is this the residence of Ida Roeder?"

"Yes, it is. Are you here to inquire about piano lessons?" the woman asked, nodding toward Emma.

Dillon cleared his throat, gave Emma's hand a squeeze, and replied, "Yes, we're here to inquire about lessons."

They were beckoned into a long entrance hall. "She's with a student right now, but if you don't mind waiting, she'll be finished soon." Following the woman's lead, Emma and Dillon found a bench outside a door through which faint notes of a Tchaikovsky piano concerto could be heard. "Make yourselves comfortable. She shouldn't be long."

The music ended in the room across from where they waited, and the mummer of voices became louder. They heard steps approaching the door, which opened to reveal a tassel-haired boy. He was followed by a woman dressed all in black who said, "See you next week, John. Practice that one section."

Emma stood as her mama turned to face her and Dillon. For a moment, their eyes met with no discernable change. Then Ida turned. "Dillon, what a surprise! Where did you come from?"

Dillon stepped forward to embrace Ida. "I came to find you. You disappeared after leaving Boise." As he gave her a quick peck on the cheek, he whispered in her ear, "I've been worried about your whereabouts." Stepping back, he gave a wink and said, "You look beautiful, as usual."

"And Emma's with you." Ida gestured, slightly flustered. She raised her hand to stroke the goosebumps popping up on her arm. "How nice of you to visit. Let's go into the parlor where we can be comfortable. I'll order tea, or would you rather coffee?"

"Tea," answered Emma and Dillon in unison.

As they sat waiting for the tray to arrive, Emma noticed that her mama had arranged her hair so that the scarred features on her face were hidden by carefully placed waves of hair. She recalled Jamie telling her about rescuing Liz from a fire, but she couldn't recall the details. That was when she'd learned Liz, Jamie's sister, suffered from amnesia. Why hadn't she put two and two together way back in Emmett and figured out Liz might be her mother? She'd felt fatigued and disoriented when she first sighted Liz months ago, never connecting her physical reactions to any possible connection to her mother. She'd returned to Santa Fe before making any link between Liz and her lost mama. If anyone else had, they'd failed to enlighten her.

Deep in thought, Emma failed to notice that Dillon and her mama were conversing. Suddenly she tuned into their conversation as Dillon was explaining he'd found her by watching all the city parks.

Laughing, Ida glanced quickly at Emma and back to Dillon. "I guess you know me better than I thought. Walking became my escape after San Francisco and my amnesia. When I was discouraged about my recovery, walking became my refuge."

After returning their empty cups to the tea tray, Ida turned to Emma. "I understand you lost your family during the San Francisco earthquake, like me. I lost my whole family, a son and daughter and my husband."

Emma blanched and quickly turned to Dillon whose jaw dropped. She hasn't made the connection between us, thought Emma.

"Ida, do you remember meeting Emma in Emmett and then again in Boise at Bruno's bedside?" Dillon asked slowly and distinctly.

"Of course I recall that," said Ida vehemently. "Her papa was in a coma because of a runaway horse accident. But why bring that up?"

"Afterward, in Boise, you and Jamie took a comatose man into your home. Do you remember who he was?" Dillon asked, moving to the edge of his chair and looking directly at Ida.

"Oh, come on, Dillon, you know who he was—an indigent patient at the hospital where I played the piano once a week for the patients. The man showed signs of recovering when he heard me playing, so Jamie and I moved him into the house in hopes he'd recover. He didn't. He died soon after we moved him."

Stunned, Emma exchanged looks with Dillon, trying desperately to convey the message that she wished to leave. It was obvious that Ida had had another memory relapse. She didn't recall being reunited with her husband before his death. Although she recognized Dillon, she didn't recognize Emma as her daughter.

"I thank you for your hospitality, but I fear Emma and I must be on our way," Dillon said, rising from his chair and assisting Emma up.

"I'm ever so glad you stopped by, Dillon. Do come by again if you're in Denver," offered Ida as she opened the front door for her guests.

Chapter 33

• • • • • • • •

Our New Mexico Gal Goes Home

"I wish you wouldn't go off like this," Wolfe pleaded, standing beside Emma at the Denver train station.

Shaking her head, Emma swallowed before answering, "There's nothing to do but head home. She's forgotten me again."

"Oh, come on, Emma. You know that's not true. She's had a lapse of memory is all. Stay a few more days to see if the shock of whatever made her forget goes away."

Shrugging her shoulders, Emma looked longingly at her best friend. "There's no point in staying any longer. She's never going to come around. She never loved me as a child, and she's not going to, ever."

Encircling her in his arms and giving her a hug, Wolfe whispered to Emma, "You have me. I love you. Don't forget that."

Returning the hug, she softly said, "I love you too."

Hearing the train whistle, the pair parted as the conductor called, "All aboard for New Mexico and places in between."

Grabbing her small valise, Emma turned to Wolfe.

Reaching up, she gave him a kiss. "May the Lord keep us safe while we're apart from the other."

He tearfully responded, "Write often. I'll be home for Christmas."

She stepped up and into the train then turned to throw him a kiss. She called, "Study hard."

Midway down the aisle she found an empty seat and slid over next to the window so she could wave to Wolfe as the train left the station. Soon his blond-headed figure disappeared, and Emma sighed as she settled back for the long ride south. She felt a warm glow throughout her body as she repeated his words in her mind: "I love you." No one but her papa had ever said that to her that she could recall. Smiling broadly, she felt the tension of the last week ease. She had something very special to look forward to, a future with Wolfe.

Suddenly a voice startled her from her musings. "Pardon me, Emma. Do you mind if I take the seat beside you?" Looking up, she saw her mama standing in the aisle.

Flustered and stunned at seeing her, Emma found it difficult to answer. She finally managed three words: "Yes, of course."

"Thank you. I'm so glad I found you. I walked through all the cars hoping to find you, fearful I'd taken the wrong train. Dillon wasn't quite certain which one you'd take." Adjusting a basket at her feet, Mama turned to Emma. "I hope I haven't surprised you too much. When we last met, I had a momentary lapse of memory about who you were. Forgive me. I know it was disconcerting for you. Dillon told me. I want us to try to be friends, if not mother and daughter. How does that sound to you?"

Dumbfounded, Emma glanced at the woman beside

her and then straight ahead at the back of the seat ahead. Thoughts of past experiences with her mother rushed through her head. She felt the rejection she experienced growing up, as well as the more recent rebuff in Denver. Could she forgive and forget? At school that's what the priest taught, but Sister Una had suggested they should forgive but never forget. She'd never thought much about either one of the messages until now. What was she to do? Oh, how she wished she could discuss the matter with Papa. He'd have an answer for her.

Turning to face her mother, Emma noticed for the first time the crow's feet at her eyes, the worry lines on her forehead, the slackness in her jaw, and the wrinkles around her mouth. Mama had aged. She was dressed in a tailored black shirtwaist and plain black gored skirt, so unlike the fashionable clothing Emma remembered seeing her in as a child. *Perhaps this woman has changed,* she thought; *maybe I should make the effort to forgive.*

Pasting a half smile on her face, Emma replied, "I'm willing to try if you are."

Head bent, Ida began talking. "I was never meant to be the mother of a daughter, or, for that matter, a mother at all. I loved your papa and thrived on the attention I received from my music. I needed nothing more. When your brother was born, your aunt Maria was the one who came to the house to care for him. I didn't want to have anything to do with him. In fact, I couldn't stand the sight of my baby because of all the pain he'd caused me. Maria had just lost her baby son and could still nurse. She stayed for a while but soon had to return to the ranch to care for Uncle Fritz. Edmund went home with her for he still needed her. When you were born,

I contracted scarlet fever, so I couldn't nurse you, nor could we be in the same room together. Your papa bottle-fed you and took complete care of you until he found a nanny. We never had the opportunity to bond as mother and daughter." Mama glanced down at her lap and then back up at Emma.

"Around the time your brother was three, I realized he was musically talented, so I took an interest in developing his gift. When you turned three I saw no giftedness whatsoever in you. I know now that it wasn't your fault, but I felt cheated. I doted on your brother, but I found fault with everything you did because of your lack of musical talent. How wrong I was. Forgive me. Your papa lavished so much affection on you that I became jealous, jealous of my own daughter." At this point, Ida stopped her confession and fell silent.

Emma studied the woman beside her, not as her mother but as an imperfect individual beginning to deal with the consequences of her past immature behavior.

"I adored your papa, to the point, I think, I expected complete devotion to me and to no one else, including you. You were competition. I didn't want to live without him, and I certainly didn't think about you and your brother when I ran into that burning building. I was so wrong, so self-centered, but thankfully, after Jamie saved and cared for me over the past several years during my amnesia, I've learned what real love is all about. I've begun to see my faults and how I've hurt others, especially you. I hope you can find it in your heart to forgive me."

Chapter 34

• • • • • • •

Emma and Mama

Feeling more content than she had in a long time, Emma left her bedroom at the back of the house and started down the windowless hall toward the kitchen. She desperately needed a cup of coffee before starting the day. Entering the large family kitchen, she found Mama staring out the window above the sink. "Good morning, Mama!"

"Good morning, Emma." Turning to face her daughter, she said, "Do you know there's a strange man walking around in the house?"

"That's Fred, Wolfe's pa, who works for us as our buyer. He's just returned from a trip to Mexico."

"Oh. I was surprised when I came down for breakfast to see a man in the kitchen making coffee."

Emma smiled at her mama's reaction. "Sorry. I forgot to mention Fred. When we arrived from Denver, he was on a buying trip, and I didn't know when to expect him back because of all the political turmoil in Mexico."

"What's going on there? I haven't kept up with the news over the border."

"Mmm. I guess only those of us who live in a border state would pay any attention to what going on down here. I'm interested because we purchase quantities of goods from Mexican suppliers to sell at the mercantile. The upheaval has been going on since 1911 because of a man named Doroteo Arango, who calls himself Pancho Villa. He's kinda the Mexican Robin Hood of the twentieth century, taking from the rich to give to the poor. He's fighting to abolish Mexico's feudal system and eliminate the slavery of the *peon*."

"Sounds like a noble cause," commented Mama.

"Well, it is and it isn't. Villa doesn't hesitate to murder those who disagree with him. On several occasions, Fred has had to turn over wagonloads of goods because Villa's men demanded them as ransom for his life. It's becoming increasing more difficult to bring merchandise across the border unless we're willing to supply him with guns and ammunition."

"I hope we don't do that," answered Mama soberly.

"No. So far Fred has used his negotiating skills to solve any dispute and keep his life."

"How did Fred come to move here?" asked Mama, pouring herself more coffee.

"He and his son Wolfe moved with us when we returned to Santa Fe from Texas. Fred was a boyhood friend of Papa's. Fred's wife ran off with their hired man just after his release from prison, where he'd served seven years for killing and butchering his neighbor's pigs that routinely rooted in his garden, ruining everything. When Papa learned Fred didn't want to remain on his farm but planned to look for his wife in Mexico, where he'd heard she'd gone, Papa offered him the buyer's job so he could search for his wife and earn a living too.

Wolfe wasn't old enough to stay on the farm alone, so he naturally came with his pa."

Mama nodded, smiling before she took a sip of coffee. "So that's how you became acquainted with Wolfe, through your papa?"

"No," answered Emma, joining Mama at the kitchen table. "I met him when Oma took me to Uncle Karl and Tante Anna's ranch outside of New Braunfels. Wolfe rescued me from being swept down the river. As the only children around, we became playmates, so to speak." Emma laughed. "We called ourselves twin outcasts, because his pa was an ex-con and my papa a murderer."

"Emma, I don't think I'd broadcast that around town; people wouldn't understand. It isn't quite true that your papa murdered his brother. He and your Uncle Fritz discovered Alwin, their brother, shortly after he'd shot their sister in the family orchard. Fritz and he were escorting Alwin to New Braunfels so they could turn him over to the sheriff, but Alwin tried to escape. Your papa tried to stop him but accidently shot him. So unfortunate," sighed Mama.

"Oh, I never knew all the details surrounding the shooting. But Mama, you'd be surprised at how many lawbreakers live around here. Many here in the 'wild west' have a secret in their past. Why, even Pancho Villa hid from the authorities for years as a peaceful, law-abiding citizen in the south end of El Paso. We tend to accept others on their behavior now, not what they've done in the past."

"Yes, and how fortunate that your papa and I could move here years ago and make a life for ourselves after the tragedy."

"But it separated the family. I didn't get acquainted

with the German side of the family until after I lost you all. How miserable a time it was for me, adjusting to strangers who claimed to be family but still held a grudge against you and Papa—well, except for Oma."

"Yes, but eventually it all turned out happily, didn't it?"

"Yes, and it did for Fred and Wolfe too. Fred discovered his talent as a buyer, and Wolfe found his true calling, medicine," Emma remarked.

As Mama washed out her mug she asked, "Did Fred ever locate his wife?"

"No, but he did discover she'd returned to Texas without the handyman but with a young son."

"Oy! Did that change Fred's enthusiasm for traveling to Mexico?"

"No, Pancho Villa did that. The fighting between different factions, especially governmental officials in Mexico City, escalated. He decided it was too dangerous to continue traveling south of the border. Eventually even Pancho Villa himself fell out of favor, lost many of his followers, and was killed."

❖

After returning to Santa Fe together, evenings found Mama at her grand piano and Emma standing close by with her violin. On Saturday evenings, a devoted crowd of music lovers crowded into their music room to listen to the duo. People passing on the street often stopped to enjoy the tunes coming forth. Once while playing, Emma glanced over the heads of the guests and thought she saw Papa's smiling face. Although she watched for him every evening after that, his image never appeared again; she began to wonder if he'd been a figment of her imagination the first time. She hoped not, for she desperately wanted him to know that she and Mama had made peace with one another.

As their musical fame spread, requests for performances around the state increased, many to benefit orphaned Mexican children fleeing the unrest in their country. They signed a contract with the University of New Mexico for six concerts during the coming year to raise money for the University's music building. Their performance calendar was always filled.

Management of the mercantile keep Emma busy. The demand for supplies had doubled, and their expansion into the wool trade required increased attention. A competitor based in Albuquerque threated to monopolize the state's wool business until an out-of-state rival forced the Albuquerque firm out of business leaving Emma's smaller enterprise intact.

One day a special letter from Idaho arrived, addressed to Ida. Although it was one of many she received, she turned it over several times, hesitating to open the missive. As Emma watched, she wondered if Mama had some kind of premonition about the letter's contents.

"Open it up, Mama," Emma urged. "You'll never know what news it brings unless you open it."

"I ... I know, but what if it's unwelcome news?"

"What are you afraid of, a rejection from one of your two admirers?"

A shy smile crept across Mama's face. "Why do you say that?"

"Oh, come on. I've seen all the letters going back and forth from Idaho. I'm not blind."

Ida stuck her thumbnail under the envelope flap and opened the letter.

Chapter 35

• • • • • • • •

Celebration 1915

At Uncle Fritz and Aunt Maria's ranch, Emma's family was busy decorating for the coming celebration. The paper lanterns strung between the hacienda and the barn swayed slightly in the afternoon breeze as Maria and Emma directed the arrangement of wooden picnic tables around the patio in preparation for the evening fiesta. The fireplace, filled with piñon wood, was ready to be lit just before the arrival of the guests. The smell of the wood permeated the air. Containers of wild flowers collected by the children decorated the tables. Fiver, the latest tailless family cat, was busy chasing the many lizards up the outdoor walls.

In the morning, Fritz had driven into town to fetch blocks of ice now resting in a newly purchased metal trough, sheltered from the heat in the nearby barn. Prepared Mexican and American dishes crowded the tables inside the hacienda, ready to be brought out to the patio after the guests arrived. Anna, Papa's sister, and her husband from Texas had agreed to remain behind to supervise the preparation of the foods that required warming before the festivities. They also would light the luminarias outlining the hacienda walls before everyone's expected arrival.

After checking to see that everything was ready, Emma set off with Fritz and Maria for town. She was eager to see Wolfe, who had taken a leave from his internship to attend the family celebration. Juan would also be there having arrived several hours earlier from Fort Bliss at El Paso.

As they rode along Maria asked, "Are you getting excited?"

"Yes! I hope I have time to wash up before getting dressed. We're later than I expected," answered Emma fidgeting with her turquoise and silver belt.

Attired in their recently sewn dresses and assisted by Juan, mother and daughter stepped downed from a horse-drawn carriage in front of the hundred-year-old cathedral. Slowly they walked up the steps to the faint notes of the church organ inside. The thick adobe structure was pleasantly cool inside, where Uncle Fritz stood ready to escort the bride to the altar. Emma handed her mama her bouquet and gave her one last peck on her cheek before taking Wolfe's arm to be escorted to the front of the church.

Within minutes after they were seated, the groom entered, followed by his best man, to stand in front of the priest. Emma glanced at the two dignified men, both with slicked-back hair and sprigs of flowers in their jacket lapels. One stood slightly taller than the other, who tried to hide the mischievous glint in his eye as he glanced toward the back of the church. The other looked toward Emma, flashed her a smile, and winked.

Emma gazed at both with fondness. If it hadn't been

for them, she'd never have been reunited with her mama. She thanked God for both, even though one would play more of a part in her future than the other.

The organ music changed. Everyone stood as Mama, in her form-fitting lace gown, walked down the church aisle on the arm of Uncle Fritz. As the bride passed Emma a tender look passed between mother and daughter. Although it had taken many months to reconcile their differences, with effort by both they'd succeeded. *Today is a new beginning for both of us,* Emma thought, turning toward the altar.

The ceremony was but a few minutes in before the priest paused to ask if anyone present objected to the union. Holding her breath, Emma glanced at the best man. Silence reigned. Emma felt Wolfe take her hand and give it a squeeze. She turned to him, meeting his eyes, which seemed to draw her very being into him. She returned the squeeze.

At being pronounced man and wife, the newly married couple left the altar. As they passed, Jamie, holding Mama's hand, winked at Emma who wiping a tear from her cheek, smiled back. She felt Wolfe squeeze her hand as he whispered in her ear, "Someday that will be us."

Epilogue

● ● ● ● ● ● ● ● ●

Emma stood in her new uniform, hat, and shoes with similarly dressed ladies, ready to march up Fifth Avenue in the New York City parade. It was late 1917. Upon learning of the need for trained nurses, she'd volunteered months ago to serve in the Army Nurses Corps. Now here she was, along with others, ready to embark on a ship for France. Her thoughts turned to Wolfe, already in France at a hospital close to the front, not far from Paris. She'd said goodbye to Juan waiting for his Army orders before departing from Santa Fe. Mama had not been happy about her decision to serve in the Nurses Corps. "It's not lady like," she'd said. Her stepfather, Jamie, had not agreed and supported Emma's decision. She was comforted knowing that he would take good care of Mama while she was gone.

The army band started playing, awakening Emma from her musings. The nurses straightened their lines. "Here we go," muttered the gal beside Emma. "We're off to war."

Emma's story continues in *Gone to War*, the final volume of the *New Mexico Gal* trilogy.

Acknowledgements

• • • • • • • •

To Lee Hanson who read the many revisions of the manuscript offering suggestions and corrections as well as encouragement from start to finish. She hosted many "sleep-overs" at her home so that we could focus on the writing to the exclusion of all else.

To Evelyn Nordeen who answered my many questions regarding nursing. Her willingness to share her own experiences was very helpful and appreciated.

To Joanne and Vice Admiral M. Staser Holcomb USN (ret.) who read, made corrections and gave suggestions on the early chapters dealing with the Pacific Ocean voyage taken by Jamie and Liz from San Francisco to Seattle.

To Brenna Day who proofread the manuscript in its final stage and give valuable teenage feedback regarding wording.

To the Emmett Historical Museum staff who endured my many questions about early Emmett and recommended the book The Village that Grew that was helpful in providing facts about early day medicine and doctors in rural Idaho.

To Christine Stewart who served as editor in the final stages of preparing the manuscript for publication.

Her continued enthusiasm for the project kept me upbeat during the long hours of rewriting

To Peter Le of Archway Publishing for his help, encouragement, and assistance in the publication of the manuscript. He was a good listener to all my concerns during the process and never failed to solve the problems I encountered, going well beyond his "job description" to help.